WE ARE GLASS

SEVENTEEN STORIES

u.v. ray

WE ARE GLASS
Copyright © 2013 u.v. ray
All rights reserved
ISBN: 978-1-291-11020-3

All of the stories within *We Are Glass* are presented as works of fiction and any likeness to any person living or dead is entirely coincidental.

10 9 8 7 6 5 4 3 2 1
First Printing

Cover and Interior Art © 2013 Steve Hussy

No part of this book may be used or reproduced in any manner whatsoever without written permission from the publisher, except in the case of brief quotations embodied in critical articles and reviews.

For all queries contact:
Murder Slim Press,
29 Alpha Road, Gorleston, Norfolk.
NR31 0LQ
United Kingdom

Murder Slim Press are:
Steve Hussy and Richard White

Published by Murder Slim Press 2013
www.murderslim.com

Printed and bound in the UK by the MPG Books Group,
Bodmin and King's Lynn

one day we will be part man and part machine

we will turn our emotions on and off as we please

one day we will love but no longer bleed...

--- Introduction ---

In the era of the bland generation u.v. ray's writing bears all the flavour of a gourmet meal at the heart of the Renaissance. While formula and conformity to the tired tropes of storytelling rule the day, u.v. ray writes with fire and heart. The public palate for the prosaic ignores the extremes of literary history. Without the likes of Artaud or Swift reading falls to the common denominator of self-gratification.

u.v. ray's stories are intrinsically poetic, and he is a fine poet, one who captures the ambiguities and menace inherent in the everyday situations that people scan and ignore. He is part of the ongoing literary movement of creating the anti-environment, the anti-establishment. If you unpick what that term means, it is a challenge to the status quo, to the ruling forces, whatever they may be, the publishers grown fat on profit or the ruling parties, smug in their ignorance. And literature has always thrived on that, writers should, as Nietzsche suggested, write in blood. If you want passion and a unique voice, read this book. If you want insight and a dark suggestive rebellion, read u.v. ray's stories and his poetry.

In this collection you will read stories by an author who wants to express those moments that men and women shy away from, all those things you dare not think. As a widely published author, u.v. ray has been tugging the hem of the establishment for years. He has been creating his highly crafted, penetrating fictions and sustaining the ongoing challenge that literature represents to those smug echelons of the ignorant and the staid.

u.v. ray is by turns passionate, angered, insightful and rebellious. He is a highly eloquent creator of counter-environments, those literary places where other things may breed. One of the key strengths of u.v. ray's writing is his paradoxical mix of iconoclasm and noble articulation of the classic themes. And to understand what that means consider what iconoclasm means. It is the deliberate destruction of symbols. Great writing removes the lid from the rotting can, it challenges the false and empty symbol. u.v. ray does that with aplomb.

I first read u.v. ray in the brilliant, irreverent *Pulp Metal Magazine*. I was struck by his precise tailoring of the English language, his use of words that do not amount to a prefect trying to please the headmaster of some squalid school situated at the edge of boredom, but a writer on fire, a writer who has a message, and it is a message placed on every burning flag across the globe.

You are about to read a man of letters in the truest sense of the word. The things you thought were true may never have been so. The establishment has been buried for years. Writing exists at the edge of the world as we know it. u.v. ray's voice is undeniable, and a gratifying antidote to the tastelessness that masquerades as Art.

Richard Godwin
Author of Mr Glamour *and* Apostle Rising
richardgodwin.net

Contents

Where are the Assassins? 09
Temporary Things 15
Is This The Life? 25
Solidarity of the Damned. 31
Match Day 41
Suitcase Full of Dust 47
No Exit 55
What's Inside A Girl 69
The Rag and Bone Man 79
Woman 95
Disintegration 101
New Dawn Dies 113
An Island Somewhere 119
Never Promise Anyone Forever 125
Metamorphosis 131
Something Wonderful 139
And So We Turn To Dust 149

Cover design and interior illustrations,
by Steve Hussy

WHERE ARE THE ASSASSINS?

I trace the outline of Elena's face, running my fingertip down her delicate nose and along her slim jaw line. She is young and the texture of her skin flawless, like a pebble on the beach made smooth by the sea. She has not a single line or a scar or blemish, except for the pretty freckles speckling her cheeks. She is the colour of coffee and cream. Her sleeping head with its auburn hair cascading like a waterfall on the pillow next to me; she is truly the most beautiful thing I have ever seen. I like watching Elena as she sleeps. Sometimes when I can't sleep I lie listening to the soft rhythm of her breathing; attuning my own with hers, until I begin to drift off.

I moulded Elena myself. Created her out of clay with my own hands and breathed life into her lungs. She is an elemental, a fantasy woman made flesh. I know that she will never age: her beauty, eternal, will never wither away like a dying flower. Elena's beauty is manifest. To this I am enslaved, powerlessly drawn by the song of the siren.

Where Are The Assassins?

Last night I shaved her cunt. She asked me to do this because she thought it would create intimacy. She sat on the bath and I knelt between her spread thighs. I shaved her using soap, warm water and a razor. I patted her dry with a towel and then bought her to orgasm with my tongue.

Elena is a seer. Sometimes I sit and listen to her prophecies and estimations. I am a maniac who is destined to drag someone over the cliff with him. I am schizoid; a different person from one day to the next. I contradict myself as various shards of my personality strive for dominance. Elena wonders whether I can remember what I have said or what I have done. Elena wonders who exactly *I* am. She asserts that I hear voices in the theater of my mind, a Shakespearean performance in which I remain embroiled.

And, of course, Elena is right. I sometimes wonder who Ricky Quinn is, too.

We live as gods in emancipation. From here in the eternal of our own choosing we could cast our nets in seas of time. There is no need for money here; money is the wage of slavery. We are given only to the pursuit of freedom and pleasure. We see no horizon from this point. The sea and land are sealed to the sky with a seamless stitch.

Elena and I live in a castle. A castle atop a hill that is perpetually shrouded in diaphanous folds of cloud the colour of graphite. From here we have the potential to command lightning strikes on the world below us. We are the assassins with bullets forged from insurgence.

Where Are The Assassins?

Actually, we live on the top floor of a tower block and I met Elena in a back-street bar. But what has reality got to do with anything?

It's a reoccurring theme, an escape from the tedium of everyday existence.

You see, there will never be the revolution that I dream of. Right now in the halls of academia they are engendering a nation of docile weaklings, fattened up for the kill. Ready for whatever shit they serve up on a plate. This is a generation budding into servile acceptance. Losing is OK. We must not dent anyone's delicate sensibilities. It's all right to be a zero – you're still just as good as anyone else. Equality is an illusory concept, subtly intended to make people feel content with being toothless and immobilized.

This is a new generation to whom failure and loss and domination by unworthy powers is to be accepted easily and with a stultified heart. They have removed the desire for insurrection by lowering the standards and creating a nation of educated morons. It soothes their sense of indolence. It removes the polarity between endeavour and lethargy. *Fahrenheit 451* is a reality, except they didn't need to burn books. People are immersed in endless video games these days; the ultimate pacification of the masses. Blazing rhetoric does not penetrate the ears of a Playstation generation too high on their own dopamine to wake up and smell the creeping cancer. Too anesthetized to realize the contempt in which they are held, it is as effective as if they'd been given an intravenous shot of morphine.

The government is corrupt. They already stopped everyone smoking. The next target is the pub. Then it will be your model aeroplane club, vintage typewriter enthusiasts, poetry collectives and coffee shops or Christ knows whatever else. What they fear is any kind of unity in the community. Their real target is the beating heart of society. Their target is *your* heart. They'll tear out your soul. They'll abolish hard cash as currency. They'll form their own clubs for people to join. They won't call it the Hitler Youth. They'll call it the Young Conservatives or the Labour Confederate of Upstanding Citizens or something like that. The Green Metrosexual Coalition of Do-Gooders.

You don't hit back with assassinations. You don't hit back at all. Instead you will smile and nod and shake the visiting politician's hand. You will graze dim-witted on the grasslands they have provided for you, sucking up the crud. And as the tanks roll in just go back to your television and Coca-Cola. Go and eat your McDonalds and shut the fuck up you bunch of fucking zombies. Relax, everything is under control.

Accept and consume. Now *there's* a party political slogan if ever I heard one.

Staring from the window, there is no release from the monotony of dull British streets, scarred with the contortions of so many desolate lives.

Where Are The Assassins?

*Beauty and freedom must prevail. It's time we started hitting back. Some of these people **need** assassinating. They are as cold blooded as any Peter Sutcliffe, or as putrefying as any religious fascism; hammer bludgeoning the populace into uniform consistency.*

Get rid of your radios and get rid of your televisions. They're feeding you a crock of shit.

"I may as well pack my stuff and get the fuck outta here," Elena says. "You're fucking insane."

Poor girl. She has me on a pedestal.

"Now how can you say that?" I ask. "To someone you look up to and revere."

She thinks I am something I am not. But if I mention this to her she says no, I only think she thinks that. I am an egomaniac.

I do not respond. Elena is such a card. One day I would, of course, make us both rich beyond the dreams of avarice. But for that she would have to stick around. I am her future investment. She has so little foresight. There is no getting out. Where's she gonna go and live? Guatemala?

"Anywhere away from you!" she retorts. Ha.

On and on these little confabs go. On and on while somewhere in the underworld Orpheus searches for his bride, a tornado tears along the Florida coastline, and the Titanic lies crumbling at the bottom of the ocean. What do I care? All these things happen a million miles away from me. I am here in my own little world of my own creation.

I light a cigarette. Elena says, "You're such a cunt" as she walks out the room.

I remain untouched, staring unconcernedly out the window. The clouds look grey and angry. I don't let my emotions get the better of me like she does. I read the clouds like an old Gypsy reads tea-leaves. There is a storm brewing.

I hear the front door slam and Elena is gone.

I remain unmoved. Mountains do not bow down before hurricanes.

Elena will come back. She always does.

TEMPORARY THINGS

In the club Ian had some blonde straddling him. On the black leather bench that ran the full length of the wall couples were either fucking with theatrical revelry or in various stages of reckless foreplay. Ian saw over the blonde's shoulder, through the murk of hazy spotlights, that Erin was navigating a route towards him. Ian eased the blonde off his lap.

"Sorry," he made a gesture at Erin, whose petite frame stood there completely naked apart from her high red stilettos. "Girlfriend problems," he joked. The blonde smiled and moved on to a couple nearby, forming a writhing threesome that entwined like a knot of snakes.

Erin moved onto Ian's lap, placing her knees either side of him, and ran her hands through his hair roughly.

"I had sex with you the other day, didn't I?" Ian asked, feeling stupid as soon as the words had tripped from his dim-witted tongue. He hated his penchant for stating the obvious.

"Yes," she fixed him with her big, brown eyes. "You did." She reached down and made him gasp as she slid his cock inside.

Erin and Ian took their bottles of beer and settled into a quiet dark corner where a muted red table-lamp bathed their faces in a warm hue. They stayed huddled together without interference from anyone else for the rest of the evening and walked out of the club hand in hand at around 1am.

It had started raining and it was beautiful seeing the raindrops glittering in the orange street lights. The pavements were glistening and reflective; everything slipping and melding, dreamlike as a Dali painting. Why on earth did everyone else on the street start running like pussies for their cars or the cover of doorways and shop canopies? Ian had always imagined he could happily live an uncomplicated life alone on an island to do as he pleased; free to swim in the sea, walk around naked in the rain.

The night was punctured by an eruption of colour in the spectacular window display of a florist's shop.

"Doesn't that look lovely?" Erin stopped for a second, pointing.

They were both soaking wet and Erin's chic dark bob haircut was sticking to her face by the time they reached Ian's Porsche. They listened to a little jazz music on the radio as he drove them back to his smart apartment at the Water's Edge on Sherborne Wharf.

* * *

Temporary Things

Happiness was to be found in the simple things, Ian thought. The sex clubs. Rain on the skin. We should commit ourselves without guilt only to carnal, sensory pleasures. There is nothing beyond the physical. The people who never find happiness in life are the ones searching for its meaning, some ethereal explanation. We are as a random as the stars. Yet even when you look up at them you're really looking at light from thousands of years ago travelling across the empty void of space. Ian had heard somewhere that in some cases a star didn't even exist, it died aeons ago and the event just hadn't reached us yet. But like us all, they eventually burn out leaving only an essence of their magnificence behind.

Ian had conditioned himself to cut out all the internal pondering, to eliminate asking himself all those philosophical questions. You can savour the taste of fruits without being a botanist. Intellectualism gets in the way of life, of that he was sure. There had come a time when, realising he'd left his life behind at every angle, burned all his bridges, Ian began revisiting all his old haunts, despondently living in the past. He took to drifting through life searching for long lost love affairs and moments in time that had long ago slipped from his grip. But he'd given up all the ruminating and pondering. Burning your bridges was fine providing there were more bridges left to cross in front of you. Heartbreak was just a part of life, there's no permanent immunity from it. That's why you just have to keep moving on.

Temporary Things

They sat at Ian's coffee table drinking hot chocolate as they dried off by the fire. "So what gives?" Erin shrugged with a playful yet unmistakably knowing smile. Her short skirt was riding high up her legs. She slipped off her shoes, revealing cute little painted red toenails as she stretched out and rested her feet up on Ian's lap.

"I don't feel," Ian said, placing his cup down on the table, "that we only just met a few days ago in the club." He put his hand on her bare thigh. "There's a kind of easiness between us, even just sitting in silence next to you it seems like I have known you for years. I dunno... just some connection between us, I suppose."

"Yes," Erin made a little walking gesture with her fingers. "Like... if we two strangers passed each other in the street we couldn't help but smile at each other. And afterward, you know, I wouldn't be able to get you out of my mind. After only that brief passing I'd search the city, looking to find you again."

"Like we'd been lovers in a past life or something, yep; that's how it seems to me, too."

Erin leaned over and kissed Ian on the mouth and said, "Now that I've found you, I don't think I want to be without you."

Erin stayed the night. In the morning Ian sat on the side of the bath watching her put on her make-up in the mirror before they went out for coffee at the 6/8 Kafé.

"So...you're a voyeur, too?" Erin laughed, pausing from applying her red lipstick.

Ian shrugged playfully. It made a lovely change to have a woman. The feminist types he'd had experiences with were not what he'd call sane people, they were warped reactionaries. Fuck knows what the word is for the female version of misogyny – but that's what they appeared to be. He'd rather look at a woman with red lipstick and a pretty dress any day of the week. Let there always exist gender definitions, and those that understand the beauty of them.

The 6/8 is a coffee shop on Temple Row, mostly frequented by students, a little further along from the beautiful flower shop they'd passed the night before. They could see the florist had opened up for the day and had conscientiously constructed another colourful arrangement of flowers out front of the shop.

It was a bright morning and they sat at one of the little metal tables outside where Erin could smoke. Depeche Mode on the stereo drifted out of the 6/8 Kafé's open door.

"I was thinking, you know, you don't ever have to be without me if you don't want to be," Ian told Erin. "If I've got the choice, I'll never let you go."

Erin took a last drag on her stub of a cigarette and dabbed it out in the ashtray. She beamed at him and grabbed his hand.

On the opposite side of the paved thoroughfare a skinny bearded man in a long black overcoat with a guitar performed Neil

Temporary Things

Diamond songs for loose change outside a shuttered bankrupt business.

They sat in quiet reflection, enjoying the simplicity of each other just being there. The morning sun glinted on Erin's silver earrings. Those brown eyes were big dark beautiful orbs, so pretty catching the sunlight. Although there was an undeniable sense of belonging between them, Erin was an absorbing enigma to Ian. He had no desire to unravel the mystery; he was simply content to have her beside him, he could sit and watch her for hours.

It was at that moment the bomb exploded. It had been left in one of the public waste-bins near the flower shop and detonated remotely. At first there was the sheer heart-stopping brutality of the blast, a searing flash of blinding white light accompanied by an ear-splitting sharp crack that sounded as though the sky had been ripped open. For a split second everything froze in mid-air, time itself seemed to be momentarily paralysed as the universe paused to assess what had happened. The very foundations of the city shuddered beneath Ian's feet. A strange silence then prevailed as shop windows around the source of the explosion shattered and shards of glass and splintered debris were thrust spinning through the air in slow motion. Half a dozen bodies writhed on the pavement before one by one slowly managing to struggle unsteadily to their feet.

* * *

Temporary Things

The busker was lying across the pavement unmoving, a pool of blood forming around his body that was strewn at an unnatural, disconcerting angle. Everything after the initial blast occurred in such indescribable silence; it felt like an age before the bloodied victims regained a fraction of their senses and began to panic, whimpering and running indiscriminately away from the scene of devastation.

Staff and customers spilled out of the 6/8 Kafé and stood looking about with darting horror-stricken eyes and ashen complexions.

"What the fuck happened?" somebody said. The voice seemed stark, disembodied in the unnatural quiet.

Ian sat there feeling kind of disconnected, numb; watching events unfold with what must have looked to everyone else like nonchalance. Erin threw her left hand up to her mouth and reached concernedly for Ian with her right but otherwise she didn't react. You don't. You think in terms of the theatrics you see on TV in such events, but in reality, barely anybody shows much reaction.

Ian later recalled feeling like Captain Obvious; some docile fucker sitting there quite passively and stupidly thinking something along the lines of: "Oh... so that's what it's like when a bomb goes off."

In the aftermath a choking mixture of smoke and dust breezed over Erin and Ian; carrying with it thousands of petals that had been blown into the air. A multitude of torn red, white and yellow petals came fluttering serenely down on them like confetti and gently stuck to their hair and clothes.

As the dust finally cleared there was an uneasy air of tense expectancy, everyone fearing a second blast. Traffic on Bull Street had ground to a halt, the birds had all flown and there wasn't even the slightest sound of bird song coming from the trees.

Suddenly a cacophonous siren wail began approaching from all over the city in all directions, shattering the illusion, restoring a sense of reality.

"Doesn't really matter, you know?" Erin said as they walked away together. "If you think of the history of mankind." Something approaching a smile started to form. "The sheer millions upon millions of people and any of us just one little speck amongst them. What makes us any more important than an ant?"

Ian placed his arm around her shoulder as they walked. "None, I suppose not," he shook his head gently.

"It's too unpalatable for most people to accept that their lives amount to jack-shit. But it's true."

"Well," Ian kicked a stone off the pavement into a drain. "I gave up thinking about it all. You wanna go and see a film tonight?"

"Sure. They're showing *Jules Et Jim* at the Electric."

On their way back to Ian's apartment they stopped and sat on the steps outside the town hall for a while overlooking the "Floozie

Temporary Things

in the Jacuzzi" fountain on Victoria Square. Of the people that wandered around the square, none of them had an ounce of life in their colourless faces. Life was simple for them because they chose not to think. In the grand scheme of things it didn't matter whether any of us lived or died.

Ian looked down and saw that one of the paving slabs had a large crack across it, through which a single, bright yellow buttercup had grown. Right in the middle of this city, this whole sprawling morass of grey concrete nothingness, syphilitic in every alley, a tiny, fragile emblem of life had managed to thrive; to rebel against the onslaught and fight its way into existence. It had refused to be denied. It was the flower that had slain the dragon.

For those few moments that delicate flower seemed like the centre of the universe. As transient as everything is, Ian and Erin were here right now, and nothing else mattered. Nothing else at all.

Temporary Things

IS THIS THE LIFE?

I poured my fifth or sixth shot of whisky and moved over by the window. This was just another moment in time, a brief moment of respite.

I'd been away at a work conference for the day, which amounted to twelve hours of lectures and demonstrations by the company directors and their assorted, brown-nosed minions. I referred to these things as brainwashing sessions. No wonder by the time I got home I was eager to hit the bottle. Not only were you expected to attend these brain-numbing get-togethers, you were expected to *enjoy* the experience as if you didn't have anything else to do. And most of the insidious bastards indeed toed the party line, enthusing about how brilliant it all was.

Most of them really didn't have anything better to do and were positively dancing with the excitement of it all. They didn't even want to get home when the tedious "summary of the day" was

Is This The Life?

finally all over; that last session when they make sure every point covered during the long, laborious day is nailed home once and for all before you were sent packing with a commemorative prize – a pink, plastic wristband bearing the company logo.

The company, they told us, was declaring war on its competitors. Some rock music blasting out the wall of speakers declared that *everyone else must die* as bottles of Champagne were handed out to individuals deemed to be of outstanding calibre. The five-hundred or so employees went into whooping and clapping raptures. This company manufactured toilet tissue, for Christ's sake. Whatever the fuck there was to be so passionate about was completely lost on me. Some of these cunts had even chosen to stay overnight, socialize with each other at the company disco held later that night in the Tokyo Suite at the hotel. No doubt they'd all roll out the tissue and have some sort of ass wiping party together.

I observed that the company did not evidently employ black people. Out of five-hundred unwiped assholes there was but one black girl amongst us.

"They don't even get interviews," one of the big cheeses laughed arrogantly when I mentioned the seeming disparity.

I just want to go away somewhere. I just want to go away and live in a little windswept, secluded house by the sea all on my own away from everything and everyone. I think the sea is beautiful but that life itself is all too sad. All our time disappears, it's all just gone.

Gone. And in the end we have nothing but formless memories like little disposable nuggets of digital data stored on a computer. There's nothing of real substance to any of it. Pleasure in this life is all too fleeting.

"OK. *The Supermarket Scenario*," the tall speaker said, pinpointing me from the stage, "You've got a shelf, and on that shelf you've got a loaf of bread, a packet of peanuts and some strawberry jelly. Now each item is priced exactly the same, so... What do you instinctively go for?"

"It depends," I replied.

"Depends on what?"

"Whatever I need at the time."

"So... just tell me. What is it you'd be most likely to need?" The stage lights were reflecting off his sweating bald head.

"Well, in that case, I'd say the jelly," I retorted confidently.

"Why on earth would you go for that?"

"Because... well, I might be making a trifle."

"But let's say you weren't making a trifle?" He seemed to be becoming exasperated.

"Well then I'd probably look at the jelly and decide that I was *going* to make one."

The speaker looked away from me clearly trembling with anger and continued talking as he paced across the stage: "The fact is *most* people would go for the loaf of bread. Such things are life necessities." He compounded his point by stabbing the air with his finger whilst flashing another angry glare in my direction. He was attempting to transmit the telepathic message: come to heel, boy.

"YES!" the crowd all intoned, "THE LOAF OF BREAD!"

Their faces were those of typical docile underlings, expressionless. Fucking bunch of fucking maggots. Not an ounce of insurrection in them.

I switched off, not really listening to the rest of the director's speech. Suffice to say, I doubted he'd be asking *me* any more questions.

This country is doomed.

Nothing feels like it is part of me anymore. I look at my clothes tossed on a chair or hanging on the rail and they do not retain a modicum of my shape. They don't feel like they belong to me, it's as if they belong to another man from another time and another place. I do not fit into this world. I can look out of my window and Birmingham looks spectacular, bursting with life, just like all big cities do when they're lit up at night. But you go into them, walk the streets, and they lose their sparkle. You just see the same dead lives behind the same dead eyes. The same rubbish blowing about the streets. The same cracks in the pavements. Most people are born and simply proceed to exist through necessity because there's nothing else to do but endure the pain. No one chooses to be born, it's all random. It's just more machine-gun discharge of disposable data.

Is This The Life?

I drink most nights. I realize you cannot run away from anything forever but it does offer a momentary escape. When you drink at least you can open up a clear lead for a short while and life doesn't have you by the throat. I rarely get up and start banging them back at eight in the morning, although there have been many times when I have wanted to.

I sat down in the armchair by the window and put my feet up on the coffee table. *Tomorrow morning I should just go ahead and do it.* When you view the world as bleakly as I do the only solution is to drink yourself into obliviousness. I just resist the need to do so at times, that's all. I am no alcoholic but I like to get the drink down me and kill as many brain cells as possible to numb myself of everything the world wants me to feel. I will be the final arbiter of what I choose to think and feel, not anyone else.

Beyond the city blocks crimson bubbled beautiful on the horizon as the death-throes of the day's sun fizzled away. The synthetic light of the city slid through the window and made the ice cubes in my whisky twinkle like stars on a flat-calm lake.

Is This The Life?

SOLIDARITY OF THE DAMNED

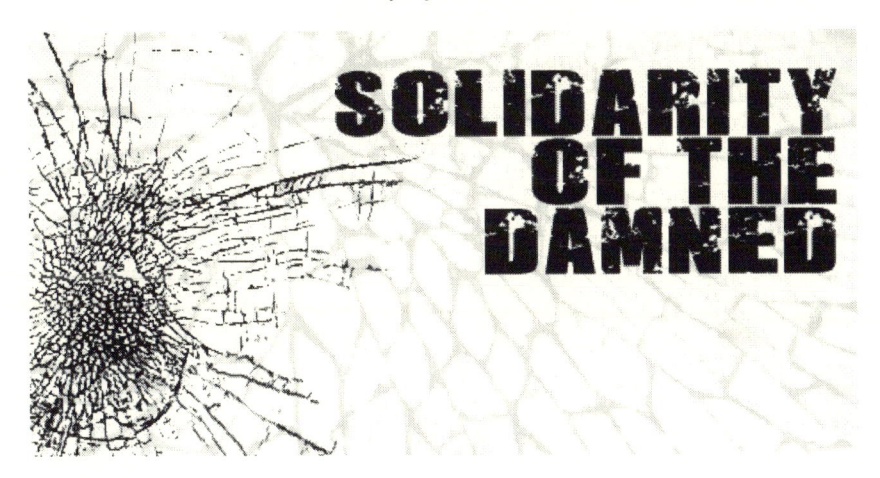

PC 7032, Martin Strurgess, was the first on the scene. The dead man was slumped over the table he'd apparently been writing at. The officer's first duty was to secure the scene and put in the call to the coroner's office. A cursory scan of the room revealed no indications of foul play, there was no sign of any struggle but these things were always such a laborious task and had to be done by the book.

The neighbour who'd called the police had come running from his house to meet Sturgess, agitated with excitement at the situation. The small, bald-headed fellow with half-moon reading glasses said the occupant, whom he hadn't seen coming or going for days, was Frederick Cireman.

"A hopeless drunk," the neighbour informed him as Sturgess shouldered the shabby front door open and entered the musty smelling property. "Though at one time quite a famous classical composer, by all accounts," the neighbour continued to shout down the hallway.

Solidarity of the Damned

The composer's name meant nothing to Sturgess.

The cold, small room at the rear of the house was sparsely furnished. A table and chair, shelves of books. Ill-fitting yellow curtains hung in the tiny window that looked out over the shambolic back yard and beyond that, the tower blocks of Birmingham. That was just about it.

Frederick Cireman was slumped over the table, a string of solidified saliva hung like a tiny icicle from the corner of his mouth from where early signs of decomposition had begun to eat away at the flesh. Scattered about in front of Cireman were numerous sheets of musical paper on which he'd been composing in pencil. Sturgess leaned over - being careful not to touch anything - and sniffed the glass of clear liquid next to Cireman's head along with a cigarette stub in an ashtray. The drink was certainly vodka. There was an orange coloured pencil, the end chewed on, lying on the floor next to Cireman's foot with its nib broken.

* * *

His vision was out of focus. He could focus his eyes if he wanted to but he preferred to simply sit there, catatonic with the room all a blur around him. Lethargic, blissful. He could hear the constant sound of the city in the distance. There was the noise of traffic. But it was no one single thing. It was traffic and it was everything else as well. It was a constant amalgamation of sounds that formed the throbbing transmission of the city. Like the heat of a summer's day, it was just there, simmering. Life palpitating, striving for supremacy like diseased cells breeding in a Petri dish.

Frederick Cireman's last opera, *The Emperor of Lozells*, had been slated by the critics. He acknowledged he wasn't what he used to be. His muse had deserted him long ago. He no longer had any idea who she even was or what had become of her. He knew nothing of the world she now resided in.

Miranda was like a viper, her pretty colours concealed venom. She was a predator; a collision of beauty and viciousness. Vicious because she did not prey for purposes of survival but out of a misplaced malice. She would perceive the slightest ambiguous or even innocuous comment as a laser-guided insult. She viewed herself as sensitive but was in fact crippled by narcissism. There was no reasoning with her.

Miranda's sexual exploits provided her with no real inner satisfaction, they were exercises intended to bolster her fragile ego. In her affiliations with other human beings Miranda floated from one to the next, seeking fulfillment, but instead leaving in her wake broken love affairs and broken people scattered around the globe.

Like many a man before him, Frederick had been sucked into Miranda's void. Frederick thought he would be the one to save her. In truth there was an ultimate sadness about Miranda. But like all those other men, he'd been left damaged. She had left him feeling alone.

The insanity of it was that in many ways Miranda was the same as he was. She sought beauty in life. The kind of beauty that

Frederick had concluded simply did not exist. Maybe it boiled down to the simple fact he had given up the quest and she hadn't?

Frederick was now just burned out ashes with only a few embers left alight. He had no idea about anything anymore. And yet still he felt compelled to sit at his table trying to compose.

"And really, for what?" he wondered. *"What the fuck for?"*

The piece Frederick was working on was to be titled *Solidarity of the Damned*.

He had lived his life through his compositions. All he ever wanted was for it to count for something. He wanted every little moment, every little second of his life to be somehow embossed into the ether. It was as if he had scrawled each note with his own blood. And yet still no one would ever know or understand his true meaning. He wasn't sure if he knew it himself; when he listened to his own completed works it was if it had come from somebody else, some disembodied entity.

We can never traverse the contours of someone else's mind, he thought bitterly.

In never being able to share Frederick's subjective experience of the world who could ever really understand the essence of what he'd been trying to create, the essence of his being? We are all bound by being alone, by such pitiful narcissism, and that, he solidly believed, had proved to be an inescapable source of anguish.

Solidarity of the Damned

At the peak of his success he had found himself once so proudly in front of the Birmingham Philharmonic conducting his most successful opera; a three part symphonic poem based on Henry Miller's Rosy Crucifixion trilogy of the same name, *Sexus, Plexus & Nexus*. But those days had all but faded away.

He'd burned himself out and was all but finished at the age of forty-nine. He could feel the lifeblood ebbing from the wounds he had suffered in life, leaving him weaker by the day. The thought brought a wry smile to his face.

On the mantle he kept stacks of his notebooks, on top of which his glasses sat. He heard the horn of a passing car break the silence of his room. Now these little things might seem meaningless. But they were passing moments in his life that no one would ever know anything about. Ah, maybe he brooded too much on these inconsequential matters. But life itself, for the most part, was nothing more than a sequence of disregarded moments. Like the passing face of a beautiful girl at the window of a train as you stand on the platform. A moment gone forever.

He drew himself out of his little reverie and looked out the window. Everything slid back into view. Grey British skies, as usual. The Rotunda thrust against the skyline. The throbbing collective heart of the city that he no longer felt any connection with.

The vodka tasted bitter, making him wince. It was a strange kind of pleasure.

Within the pages of those notebooks he would record thoughts as they came to him. Memos, diatribes, lists, short bursts of musical notation that he'd later expand upon.

He tried to allow his work to grow organically. He drew on autobiographical subject matter and his observations of the world. His overall ethos was to present the average man as elite, to elevate those designated as proletarians to their rightful place above the lazy, ineffectual, parasitic aristocracies that preside over us by right of birth.

His personal conviction was that within society there was born a natural hierarchy, and that natural hierarchy identified itself by its deeds rather than its bloodline. Within the sprawling morass of humanity there are worthless parasites, there are adequate individuals, there are exceptional individuals. And forming the fountainhead, there are those who walk amongst men as Gods.

This Nietzschean philosophy of Frederick's was probably one of the reasons he didn't sit well with the critics on their intellectual high horses and moral high grounds. In fact, he laughed to himself, it was most likely why he didn't sit well with anyone at all. But he'd never been too interested in their wishy-washy dribblings. Such zealots do not appreciate those of us who stoke the proverbial fires of hell beneath their feet.

He carried a notebook everywhere with him. The books went back years. Frederick drew on the cigarette as he laid his current notebook on the table and flipped through the pages of what he'd written, usually in drunken disarray, throughout the preceding week:

Solidarity of the Damned

...and life is brutal. And all there is brutality. All are adversaries. And if you don't knock seven bells out of someone they will knock it out of you. If they don't do it physically they will do it mentally. And this struggle is perpetual; it's the force of your will against the world. And like the old stone gods one day you are unavoidably laid to rest and no part of your physicality lives on. You become as dust. But in life such was the magnitude of your primacy no one can believe you're no longer there, fierce and raging with the fires of youth. You walked magnificent as a God amongst men.

We are an animal as any other animal. But because of our heightened awareness this gives a man the notion that he possesses moral superiority over another and thus anoints him with a passion that makes him believe he has the right to kill purely on the basis of that morality. The fight is primal. Such is the natural tumult within the society of men that it becomes as a self-fulfilling prophecy. And the victors claim their moral rights. Those who simply do not accept this code of natural ethics are the ones who will perish. God only exists in the brains of men. But those minds and the actions they instigate do indeed perpetrate their idea of God's will on earth. Their collective heart is greater than that of the individual. And it is an evil heart. A heart that does not pump blood but bile. The law cannot effectively prevent crime because it is contrary to the nature of man. In effect, we have created a society we are all struggling to fit into...

Solidarity of the Damned

When Frederick thought about a heart, he didn't consider anything ethereal or spiritual or of love and emotions. He thought of only blood and muscle and tissue with every pulsing spasm being one beat closer to death. Absolute death. The eternal state of nothingness that comes to us when our purpose is done and we have no remaining will with which to imprint ourselves upon the fabric of reality.

...We have lived entombed by laws established on grounds of religious morality. This is the age of dissent, where those laws are breaking down. The laws of the enthroned hierarchy are illusions, a fallacy. These laws acquiesce to the true bestial nature of man, for within mankind there lurks a beast that can never be fully contained. No religion or political ideology has ever succeeded in quelling the true spirit of man. Even intellect itself is pulverised in the vituperative pursuit of his own base emotional gratification because such gratification is as central to man's survival as is water....

Frederick's thoughts were of darkly foreboding violins. Marching percussion; *drumming drumming drumming*. A pounding, relentless coming of the shadow of death across the face of the earth, until the irrevocable holocaust, leaving only ripples of tranquillity until finally there is nothing but the delicate plucking of harps, as if we had never even existed at all.

Solidarity of the Damned

In the final analysis, we don't even possess the strength of strings.

We are glass. We are all so easily broken.

As Frederick fell forwards clutching his chest with his left hand, the pencil slipped from the grasp of his right. With his head on the table, breath wheezing in his tight chest, he watched sideways as it rolled across the surface and clattered to the floor.

* * *

Impatiently waiting for the arrival of the coroner PC Sturgess lifted one of the notebooks from the mantle and opened it at random.

In pencil scrawled down the page was a shopping list:

Peas,

Potatoes,

Washing-up liquid,

Milk,

Vodka (4 bottles, cheapest kind).

Solidarity of the Damned

MATCH DAY

Dogmeat's bedroom window overlooked the children's play area just across the road. On summer evenings gangs of teenagers hung out there. The young girls would often sit on the park bench in their little short skirts talking and laughing with the boys. As the sun sank below the horizon to the west the over-sexed little bitches would blatantly sit there with their legs gaping open, thighs golden in the sunset, begging for it. Dogmeat was able to camouflage himself behind his nets and see right up their knickers. With a telephoto lens he could sneak a really good crotch-shot. He made no secret of the fact he had a photo-album full of such surreptitiously snapped pictures.

"You shoulda seen this one," he drooled, cupping imaginary breasts in his hands. "Blonde. About seventeen. I tell you, I'd shove my tongue up her ring-piece and leave it there furra month! Jeez, I would. I'd count every hair on her cunt and count 'em again to mek sure I hadn't missed one."

Match Day

Dogmeat was in his fifties, maybe fifty-four or five. He had a gold tooth at the front that glinted amidst his row of yellow ones. He'd got an ex-wife floating about somewhere in his past with whom he had spawned the next generation, a son he'd named Dwight.

Today he got on the train wearing his Birmingham City football shirt and a big, chunky faux gold chain around his neck. It was pissing down and rain pounded against the roof of the carriage and ran down the windows. Dogmeat spotted me and made a bee-line down the aisle towards me. Half his face was bandaged up and his one eye was black and swollen.

"What happened to you?" I asked, as he thumped down heavily in the seat beside me.

"You know the Tavern in the Town? Yeah, having a few pints in there, like, and a couple of niggers chucked me through the front window," he said, chin raised with a certain amount of pride. I didn't ask to know anything more. I didn't need to. I already knew. Dogmeat was a racist and always liked to get right up in their faces and tell such people repeatedly they are monkeys. I don't know what he was trying to prove but he was always getting battered for such behaviour. He'd goad them and goad them until someone finally snapped and banjo'd him. Not even because they were offended, or that he'd stumbled upon a morsel of truth, touched a nerve – but just because he was an annoying little prick.

"We're at home to Everton," he said excitedly, pointing in the direction the train was travelling. "Can't wait. Premier league now, man." He drummed agitatedly on the back of the seat in front of us with both hands; tasteless gold sovereign ring on every single finger, even the thumbs, clinking together. "So, Where you watchin' the game, Chief?"

"Don't really watch football," I shrugged.

"We're gonna struggle to stay up, you know? Mind you, Robbie Savage – he's your man." Dogmeat scrunched up his mouth and rocked his head emphatically. His ruptured face looked like a grotesque Francis Bacon painting. "Robbie Savage... top of the pops, Squire. But I don't think much of *that* Caribbean fool we've got. What you reckon?"

"Yeah." I nodded, without a clue who he was talking about.

Is it really a fact that ninety-five percent of the human race do not think? That all ambition has been wrung out of them? Here's your McDonalds. Here's your MTV. Now have a nice day and shut the fuck up.

We are just pigs in shit. And we have no greater aspirations than this. Placated working class suburbia, drip-fed a diet of inconsequential fucking bullshit does not pose a threat. It ensures whole nations of docile underlings remain exactly that. It may well explain why we keep voting the jackasses in. There will be no kicking in of the doors behind which our leaders sit conducting their underhand dealings. For the first time in history, the state is insurmountable. The revolution ain't gonna happen. Just put your X in the box. Keep your snout in the trough and keep sucking up the crud. Thank you for your vote. This general election has been sponsored by Coca-Cola and brought to you by Sky Television Entertainment.

Dogmeat was just another one of the ten-million have-nots sucked right into the system, hook line and sinker. Every two weeks, signing on the dole. He had no chance. He didn't fucking want one. He'd never worked a day in his life. Actually that's not true. What I should say is he's signed on the dole for all his adult life. He works intermittently. Cash in hand, fitting upvc double-glazed windows and doors.

"Don't get thinking if it wasn't for people like me you'd be paying less tax. If it weren't for people like me they'd just find another way of taking it off you," was always his excuse. And of course, on that score, Dogmeat was absolutely spot-on. "I play the system for every fuckin' penny I can get out of them bastards."

I hopped off the train at a crowded New Street Station; people all over the place with their ratty little faces, pushing and shoving, scurrying about like mad things. I suddenly imagine all those immense peaks and troughs carved into the ocean beds. And because most of us will never experience it, because we will never stand on the cusp of the abyss; we have no comprehension of how small and insignificant we are. The world ends at the parameters of our own egos, at the end of the street, at the boundaries of our own parochial little towns.

The whale has the ability to create within its brain a complete 3D map of the whole oceanic world around the planet. All those peaks and troughs perused and memorised in minute detail. Unlike

Match Day

the whale, people become embroiled in trivial dramas of our own making. We don't know where we started from or where the hell we're heading. Staring up at a night sky each star is another world, another point of consciousness we can never know. Each raindrop beading down the train window, throbbing with cell life. And within each cell a single thought, a solitary impulse, the desire to evolve. The desire to live and to stare into the void and say: I am more than just a speck of light in the eye of death. I am another universe.

But I digress. Maybe I think too much. Perhaps I am a prisoner of my own neuroses.

Amid the bustle of the station I expected the announcement to come over the Tannoy at any moment: "The trains are running on time today, ladies and gentlemen. Relax. Everything is under control. Everything is running smoothly. Life is sweet. Just keep sucking on those cigarettes."

Match Day

SUITCASE FULL OF DUST

I was in a car crash yesterday. I watched the driver die. But I lucked out of it without a scratch. It made no difference to me; I couldn't have given a fuck. It's not like I knew the guy who'd picked me up. I climbed out of the over-turned wreck and lit a cigarette, waiting for the ambulance or police or whatever to arrive. I stood about by the side of the road smoking, watching the sky cloud over. I thought we were going to have yet another summer storm but the rain managed to keep off for once and it soon cleared up again in no time at all. The evening was peaceful and serene.

The driver was called Keith, a corporate computer sales rep from the North-East somewhere. I forget exactly where he said he was from, but it was somewhere up there. It doesn't matter. His side of the car took the full impact. His body smashed to a pulp right before my eyes. We'd just pulled off the motorway where he was going to drop me off. He just didn't see the other vehicle, I suppose. Like I told the policeman; everything happened so quickly I don't really know what happened. Keith made a final rasp, his brains oozed from his nose and his ears and then he was gone. Simple and final as that.

I am a man who is perpetually alone. I am alone right down to the bitter sediment at the bottom of the glass. I prefer it that way these days. The endless swirl of nightclub lights holds no allure for me anymore. Every bar looks the same. Every woman feels the same.

I sit and drink alone at home. I don't expect anyone to understand. This is my method of suicide. I am fucking dead inside, I've nothing left to give and there's nothing left to take. I have burned myself out. All I have now is my whisky and my thoughts. I work a dead-end, part-time job just so I can support shutting myself away in a room with my whisky and my thoughts for as much of my time as possible.

That's how it goes. The drugs and the drink suck the fucking life out of you in the end. When you have lived too much there's nothing left to experience and you end up with your senses numbed, you're detached from the world around you. To be able to feel and to love always requires a modicum of innocence, naivety, hope, landscapes yet unconquered; you need to be still viewing the world with the wide-eyed innocence of a child in some way. You need to hold on to some fantasies, once you've explored them all there is no sense of wonder left, nothing left to live for. My body is scarred from the velocity at which I have lived. And in my mind the scar tissue has hardened and become immobile, insensitive. I am healed, but left unresponsive to stimuli. Too tough to live and too tough to die, I am caught in a kind of limbo. I watch each blood-red sunrise bleed into each blood-red sunset and in-between every vapid day just drones on the same as the last.

I'd delivered a new VW Beetle to a dealership in Carlisle and was making my way back home, thumbing a lift by the side of the motorway at junction forty-three. I had my red and white delivery plates and my sign saying BIRMINGHAM. Keith flashed past in his silver machine then stood on his brakes, stopped, and reversed back up the slip road, zig-zagging towards me, reverse gear whining painfully. He opened the window and said he could take me as far as Walsall. He was coming off at Junction 10. I said that was fine and jumped in. "I'm Keith," he said offering his sweaty hand with a smile. "Tony," I shook his hand and smiled back.

I would have expected him to start a conversation like they all do, asking what kinda cars I deliver and to where. But Keith didn't. I put the plates down in the foot well between my feet. Keith pointed at my left hand and asked straight off the bat, "Not married?"
I replied that no, I wasn't.

"Don't blame you," he spat. He had these small beady eyes that darted about shiftily; they swivelled in their sockets and reached you before his head turned to face you. As he chattered on and on his thin lips rolled back in a pained grimace, revealing his ghastly pointed little teeth that looked like they'd been sharpened with a file.

Regardless of the fact that I wasn't saying much in response Keith motored on like a madman, ranting about how he'd been the victim of a deception. All the signs were there: his wife had been cheating on him. He'd suspected it for a long time, he nodded. When she kissed him off to work in a morning he was sure he could taste another man's cock on her mouth. When he'd finally discovered the truth for certain he'd beaten her up. He waved his hands around as he spoke. He'd beaten her up "good and proper," he said, gritting his teeth and thumping the steering wheel so hard the whole dashboard shook. "Oh yeah, Christ, I made a right mess of her."

The eventual outcome was that the bitch had left him for this other man, a fucking butcher of all things. Luckily she and Keith didn't have any kids so that made it a bit easier. God alone knew the last thing a kid needs is a fucking whore for a mother. And another thing that aroused his suspicions, he said, was when she went for a bath. He was sure she was masturbating in there while he sat and watched TV. He ranted furiously about how he'd wanted to kick the door in and burst in there shouting: you want some cock? You want some cock, do you? Here... I'll give you some fucking cock! Bitch.

He asked me if I thought he'd been justified in giving her a good hiding. I told him I wasn't married and thus did not know about these things, that I couldn't speak from experience but that I was sure that kind of thing went on all the time behind the closed doors of married couples. "So I doubt it's unusual," I added, reassuringly.

He seemed pleased with that diagnosis and nodded vigorously. "It does," he enthused. "It happens all the time." He pulled out a packet of cigarettes from the breast pocket of his blue shirt, "Smoke?"

I made a dismissive gesture and told him, "No thanks."

After his wife left him Keith had suffered a nervous breakdown. That was two years ago. Knocked him for six, screwed his head up for a good six months. He couldn't believe it, there'd been no prior warning for all her bullshit. They'd had a very happy twelve years of marriage. "I was as good as gold to that woman," he bemoaned, stabbing the air with his index finger. And she repaid him by going and fucking the local shit-for-brains butcher.

"You got a girlfriend?" he suddenly turned his attention on me.

"Not any more," I said. "We split up."

I was better off keeping it that way, Keith went on. I should take his advice and keep it that way. Never get involved with the back-stabbing bitches. But I knew that. I didn't need him to tell me. I was a wise sort. Yeah, he could see that for sure.

For a while we travelled along in silence. I looked around and noticed Keith's suitcase was on the back seat. And then he started talking about his job. He was currently the company's top salesman. That's where he focused his energies nowadays. I switched off. I looked out the window at the rolling green and featureless landscape until Keith brought me back by slapping my arm, he had a huge gloating expression on his face, his sharp incisors grinning at me like some ravenous, flesh-eating little animal. It looked like Keith had hacked at his own hair in some mad fit, run a number two razor over his whole head so there was no shape to his hairstyle. It was bright ginger and stuck out in bristles like a toilet-brush, the top, sides and back equal length all over, just sticking up.

"...So," he was concluding his story. "Not only did I sell them the computers and all the software to go with it... I sold the cunts the full insurance package *and* the extended five-year guarantee. Smashed my monthly bonus." He punched the air jubilantly and shouted, "YES! GET IN! HAVE SOME OF THAT YOU BASTARDS!"

Keith then wondered whether I wanted to go to a brothel with him. He knew a great little brothel on Ablewell Street, not even two-hundred yards from the hotel where he was staying overnight in Walsall. He wouldn't normally mention it to a stranger but he felt that we were really getting along well. We could stop off for a few drinks, he knew a great little wine-bar, before filling our boots in this brothel. He enthusiastically suggested I could easily get a bus or train afterwards to Birmingham; it was only an additional twelve or so miles, after all – barely any distance at all. I shook my head and thanked him but said I didn't think so. Keith seemed flabbergasted. "It's not expensive," he continued trying to convince me. "You can get sucked off for twenty quid, and the birds are fucking stunners, man!" He held out a palm, anxiously awaiting my response. I told him again, I didn't think so.

"Ahh," Keith lamented. "Shame, I get the feeling you and I have a lot in common. I get the feeling we could be friends. It's not often you meet people who share an understanding of life. Tell you what, Tony, before you go I'm gonna give you my card; we'll get together some other time. What you say?"

I agreed that yes, we were really getting along famously and I'd take his card and give him a bell sometime. Keith beamed a big smile at this and I felt a little sorry for the sad, mad bastard.

As we approached the Walsall exit Keith was earnestly puffing on the last few millimeters of the cigarette like a maniac, getting everything he could out of it. We exited the motorway and he opened the window a touch and threw the stub out as we approached the traffic island. He didn't stop when he should have done and drove straight into the line of traffic coming from the right and... BOOM.

"That was the last thing I remember," I told the policeman at the scene. "There was a flash of white, a colossal bang, the sound of crunching metal and glass. Next thing I knew we were over there on our roof, entangled in the wreckage."

The cop surveyed the scene, looked at Keith's mangled silver Vauxhall lying on its crushed roof and the white van that hit us alongside it toppled on its side. Amongst the wreckage Keith's suitcase had been slung clear. It lay on the grass smashed open and some of what were obviously his ex-wife's clothes that he was still desperately holding onto had blown into a tree and were flapping gently in the wind. It was nothing but a suitcase full of dust, the ashes of his broken life.

"You were lucky," the policeman said. "Sure you're alright?"

"Yeah," I nodded. "I was born lucky, me."

In truth, as far as I was concerned, nothing had changed. All I wanted to do was get home and sit and get drunk. It was just another day and tomorrow would be another one. The sun was just about dropping below the horizon and the sky was streaked with glowing red aeroplane trails. There was a light, warm breeze. And for some reason the constant hiss of traffic obliviously speeding along the motorway on the other side of the embankment seemed relaxing to me. I walked in the direction of town, looking for a bus stop.

Suitcase Full Of Dust

No Exit

My day starts at 7.30 with a roll call. We're kept in our cells for this. The guards come around and make sure everyone is accounted for and everyone and everything is where it's supposed to be. Providing they account for everything being in good order, we go down for breakfast at 8 and at 8.30 we have 20 minutes of trudging around the yard, which for most of us is the only moment of reprieve we get from the foul air that blasts through the clanking steel grey wing of the prison.

Everyone goes off to their jobs just before nine. But for me this means being confined back in the wing until lunchtime. I am a new inmate and - although I have applied for a job in the workshop assembling wheelchairs and prosthetic limbs for the local health authority, for which I will get something like £5 per week - the application hasn't yet been processed and authorised. So without a job my days are currently mind numbingly dull. I have little to do until dinner at 5.30. After dinner most of the others have some free time and they're allowed to use the gym, library and other such pursuits. But for me, this means being sent to see either the drug and alcohol rehabilitation specialists or the shrink. It alternates between the two. This was deemed by the judge to be a key component of my incarceration. Their intention was to discover a morsel of humanity somewhere inside me and nurture me into a decent human being.

I have a cellmate called Danny. He's a big hefty fucker from up north with a shaved head and a blind right eye. From just beneath the blind eye a jagged scar runs around his cheek tracing a line all the way to his ear. He has a faded blue tattoo of a snake coiled around his bulging neck. We are allowed a stereo in our cell. Danny listens to *The Exploited* a lot. "Proper punk," he calls it. He's an okay bloke, I think. I don't ask what he's in for and so far he hasn't questioned me either.

When I first got in he gave me a toothbrush with a slither of razor blade glued into it, hidden in the bristles. "Little skinny bastard like you, yull fookin' need it, brutha. Trus' me," he laughed. "Keep two in yr'pocket. Jus' don't pull out the wrong 'un... ha ha ha ha... an' brush your fookin' teeth wi'it." He laughed until he hacked up a glob of black phlegm and spat it onto the floor. Danny also advised me if any twat starts any *argie-fucking-bargie* not to think twice about "opening them up." He assured me: "It's the only way yull get respect an' they'll leave you alone. You gotta put yr'self on the same par as them. Don't gi'em the first fookin' shot, jus' slash the cunts one. I'm tellin' you, slice their bastard ears off."

Danny also tells me he can get his hands on some billy or a bit of blow, skag if I want that shit. He was my man. All I have to do is give him the nod.

So this is where I am right now. But let's go back.

* * *

We drank Night Nurse a lot, me and Trip. In liquid form that cough medicine, supplied with its little measuring cup, resembled methadone in a spectacular way. Night Nurse is an antihistamine notorious for its powerful sedative side effects; and we used it expressly for the purpose of sedating ourselves – drinking it straight from the bottle. It also contained dextromethorphan; a drug that causes euphoria and hallucinations due to its effect on the central nervous system; acting on the body's principle receptors. You didn't even have to drink a serious amount. I mean this green liquid was so fucking good I couldn't believe it could be purchased legally over the counter without prescription. I don't recall a pharmacist ever seriously questioning their customers about what they wanted certain medicines for, not in those days. They seem to have tighter policies on such matters nowadays.

We usually went in early on a Saturday evening and bought three bottles each. I would call it naivety, but two skinny-looking speed-freaks walking into an all night chemist's and buying bottles of the stuff was obvious enough to anyone. But we used those dirty city chemists you find on the edges of town with red neon signs in

No Exit

the windows, open 24 hours and situated next door to dirty taxi offices and kebab joints. They'd sell almost anything to anyone with either minimal enquiry or, more usually, with utter nonchalance and resignation. It was a cheap and easy high on its own but of course we always mixed it with any other drugs we could get our hands on.

"Thing is, Shoe," Trip said. "Ain't gonna be long before they cotton on to the fact that kids like us are drinking the stuff for fun. Then the bastards'll take it off the fuckin' shelves or make it a prescription drug or something." But that possibility didn't particularly bother us either because we had Guss.

Guss could get us anything. Aside from the speed and acid he also got us prescription strength morphine or codeine. Quite often he'd chuck us pills and we had no idea what they were; we'd just swallow them without fear or question. Guss's place was like an apothecary. Shelves stacked with big sweet jars full of colourful pills and potions. For as long as there were shoddily run chemists and people like Guss, getting drugs was like shooting fish in a barrel.

Guss was more than twice our age. I think he once mentioned being 50-odd but it was hard to tell because he was so wizened he looked even older, knackered beyond belief. He played drums in our band, *The Queen-Mother Slags*. Trip was lead guitar and vocals and I played bass. Trip at least had a Strat. A nice blue one. A classic '57. Fuck knows how a scuzzball like him acquired it. Myself, I had some piece of shit Avon Rose Morris bass that I took a paint brush to and jazzed it up by scrawling *Queen Mother Slags - Underground Heavy Groovin'* across its paint-chipped body. I'd never even heard of the fucking things but I bought it for ten quid in a junk shop along the same street as my flat in Erdington. I tuned it right down, strings all loose. It gave me a rough, dirty sound and fed through a turbo-distortion pedal turned up to max it hardly mattered what I played.

Guss looked like an old hippy type. He dressed in a lot of suede and corduroy like the remnant from the 60's that he was. He became the drummer after I met him at a bar. He always wore a red beret with his grizzled long grey hair hanging from under it down to his shoulders. Guss had done so much acid over the years he couldn't keep his eyes still. His pupils jittered about quickly from side to side like amoebas pulsing under a microscope.

Guss had played in various garage bands over the years and wasn't just a good solid drummer; he was a truly creative musician. The way he attacked the drums, weaving his own little flourishes and idiosyncrasies into the rhythms always reminded me of Clem Burke or Keith Moon. He was wasted in The Queen-Mother Slags. But Guss had missed his boat years ago. Fucked himself up on acid and Christ knows what else.

The 80's had come to a close and the new decade begun but the decor in Guss's living room at his flat looked like it hadn't changed since the early 70's. Red leather sofas with chrome legs and faux leopard skin throw-overs were arranged around the perimeter. Over in one corner he had a massive yucca plant that sprouted from its pot into the centre of the room where the top of it had to be supported by a cord fastened to a hook in the ceiling. Guss claimed he'd been growing the yucca for 25 years.

No Exit

On the dusty shelves amongst a vast collection of vinyl, Guss had disco lights that bathed the room in shifting hues. It was a dreary, brown looking block of flats he lived in and I suppose all that swirling psychedelic lighting created an atmosphere that concealed the less palatable reality of crumbling plaster and rotting woodwork that was still apparent from the constant smell of damp.

Together we were an odd and befuddled ensemble. Trip and me had no real idea what we were doing. We could just about hold together simple repetitive rhythms swept under a carpet of reverb and distortion but that was our limit. We made a noise and labeled ourselves under the banner of punk. The band was just an escape from the drudgery of everyday existence. Trip had this little yellow Ford Escort van that we couldn't fit much in. It was just the three of us with the Avon and the Strat, a drum kit, three or four Marshall amps and the peddles.

I suppose we had our dreams for The Queen Mother Slags, nigh on impossible as it was they'd ever see fruition. We even concocted stage names. Due to his poor eyesight Guss was Mr. Magoo, Trip was Bertie Boop and I was The Shoe.

My black Cuban-heeled Chelsea boots were always highly polished; unless I'd given someone a good kicking in a brawl and gotten blood over them. Those pointed toes and heavy heels had come in handy in many of the rough clubs we'd played in. You don't get a name like The Shoe for nothing. I enjoyed playing in the band but I enjoyed giving someone a good shoeing even more.

No Exit

We'd visited the chemist shop earlier that afternoon.

"Who exactly wants all this medicine?" asked the pharmacist behind the counter, peering over her half-moon glasses at Trip who was standing conspicuously hunched over with his spiked green hair and nose stud, sniffing profusely like he'd been snorting coke all morning.

"I do," I stepped in, slapping a twenty in her palm. "I'm stocking up. Gotta beat this flu bug that's been going 'round, you know?" I stuffed my 3 bottles in the pockets of the green USAF jacket I was wearing and we sauntered out of there.

Guss poured the whiskey and handed out E's. I usually took my whiskey straight but I was mixing it with the Night Nurse and swilled two tabs down with it. We had a gig that night at a place in Walsall called the Wheatsheaf, opposite Blue Coat School. When we had a gig we always used to sit in Guss's place and spend the afternoon psyching ourselves up by getting out of our skulls.

Guss had cats. I don't know how many cats he had but there were a lot and each time you visited his place there seemed to be countless numbers of them creeping out from under and behind the furniture. It was a first floor flat and Guss had constructed this rickety wooden ramp that ran from an always open freezing rear window and down the wall to the ground outside.

The flat had a constant infestation of fleas. You'd come away with flea bites around your ankles and up your legs. But Guss claimed he didn't have an infestation. He had a method of dealing with them. There might be one or two, he told his constant stream of visitors coming to buy drugs, but the place wasn't infested.

"Ensuring a perpetual high level of alcohol content in the blood provides round the clock protection," he expanded. "They're the hardest creatures to defend against," he flicked a strand of grey hair from his face with an air of authority.

"Not as hard as a lion," Trip butted in.

"Yeah, they are, ahh, see!" Guss retorted, waggling a corrective finger. "Shoot the balls off a lion. You can't shoot what you can't see, man." He shook his head emphatically. "Greedy little bastards that they are, one flea can bite up to 300 times during the night. And they breed so fast each female can shit out... get this... *can shit out 10,000 eggs in a 9 day life-cycle*." He squinted, seriously. "They lay 'em in the carpets, see?"

Guss said he'd studied the subject thoroughly. "They're like the Russian army: pissin' millions of 'em." He swept a finger over the room. "Deployed in strategic positions in a very short space of time."

Trip scratched his calf ardently.

"Yeah... they go for your legs usually," Guss conceded, swigged his whiskey. "But I sort the little cunts out by drinking a bottle of whiskey before I roll into bed."

"Yeah," on Guss's blind side I winked at Trip. "Let them suck on that!"

Trip threw his head back and laughed mockingly

No Exit

"Ha ha. Exactly!" Guss persisted. "I've estimated it's possible to wipe out an army of 10 million fleas in only 3 weeks of consecutive night's whiskey consumption." He sparked up a joint and pointed with it. "I reckon that green shit you're drinking would do the trick as well."

Guss's darting little amoeba eyes flickered in the multi-coloured lights. He drew deeply on the joint and passed it to me across the glass coffee table, tightening his lips to keep the smoke down. In turn I took a couple of deep drags and handed it over to Trip's awaiting hand that was stretched out like a baby bird's beak to its mother.

After polishing off the Night Nurse and whiskey cocktails I was feeling... indistinct. But after about half an hour the haziness was counteracted when the disco biscuits started kicking in and lethargy was punctuated by periodic sudden rushes of blood to my head. I felt as though the world around me was alternating between slow-mo and fast forward. When the time came to load up the van with our gear my head was reeling so much I could hardly get up. But since we were such a rudimentary outfit to call it loading up was an exaggeration. We slung in the gear in 15 minutes and made a move.

Trip struggled to hold a straight line as we headed along the Birmingham Road into Walsall. "Can't see a fucking thing!" he slurred, wrestling the steering wheel as if he was fighting a slippery eel, swerving heavily left to right as car horns blasted at us from every direction.

I was rolling about with the gear in the back. Guss sat next to Trip in the passenger seat. "You just press the fuckin' accelerator," Guss ordered, leaning over, grabbing the wheel. "And I'll steer."

We travelled like that, the pair of them sniggering and sharing a half bottle of vodka until we reached the Wheatsheaf. We lurched to a halt with one front wheel crashed up on the curb and we all staggered out onto the pavement outside the place. It was about 7pm and there was a group of straggle-haired indie kids standing outside with their beers. Secretly impressed, they started snorting at us as we fell about trying to lug the stuff inside and thumped up the staircase to the upstairs room.

We got set up and then sat at the bar having a couple more beers before kicking off about 9pm. It was a full house. People had piled raucously into the small room and started chanting.

We kicked off with Trip bellowing: "HAVE A BIT OF THIS, YOU WANKERS," as we launched into our first number, *Sleek Black Cadillac*. We managed to get through two shambolic renditions of songs before the spitting started and glasses were hurled towards us. A few stray missiles slammed into the optics at the back of the bar and sent shards of glass spinning. The barman quickly rolled down the shutters. We attempted to play through the rampage but even our Marshall amps were drowned out by the

No Exit

shouting and Trip and me had unstrapped our guitars and were using them to bat away the screaming projectiles as Guss cowered behind his kit. He was pulling faces at the crowd, goading them on and laughing.

Some thick-set skinhead came towards me gritting his teeth and lunged at me with the serrated remains of a pint glass. I took hold of the bass and thrust the machine heads hard into his face. It ripped his cheek wide open, red raw like a piece of bloody steak. He slumped heavily to his knees with his head in his hands. Blood pumped out through his fingers and poured down his patchy bleached denim jacket. His broken teeth fell onto the floor in front of him. He rolled onto his side and I swung again, axe-like, chopping the instrument into his ribs. The room had frozen around me and everyone watched in dead silence as I stood over him and pressed my boot into his throat. He was trembling uncontrollably and he held his hands up and whimpered simply, "stop."

I brought the Rose Morris down, smashing it hard in his face. It shattered his cheek bone. The cunt apparently had to have a steel plate inserted to rebuild his face.

* * *

So here I am serving my first jail term. 6 months for GBH. My defence got me off a charge of malicious intent on account of the fact that my first attack - ramming the machine heads in the skinhead's mouth - was in self-defence against someone brandishing a weapon. It was for sustaining the assault when he was down that I'd gotten the charge of GBH. It started in self-defence and apparently turned into the act of a psychopath. The judge said I was a nut-case and referred to it as, "the actions of a not particularly intelligent young man." But as anyone who's been here knows, the justice system is all a game. Life itself is a game of Monopoly. Round and round the board we trudge. Our characters are defined, cast in iron. There's nothing we can do about who we are. We are at the mercy of the system, they set the rules, and that's all it comes down to. Go straight to jail. Do not pass Go. Do not collect 200 pounds.

They say the hardest part of prison is being away from your family. I don't have a family to speak of. I mean, I have a biological family of course. I just never speak of them. There were no excuses. I didn't have a hard or difficult childhood. In fact, my parents were quite wealthy. They lavished attention on me. Sent me to the best private schools and gave me everything I wanted. And in doing so, they created a monster of insensitivity. I've never been able to empathise with other people in any kind of human capacity. I'm trapped inside myself. An island from which there is no exit. I'm not exactly crazy, but all it takes is the right sequence of events to drop into place like the tumblers in a lock and I'll just stick a knife straight through you.

Psychiatric reports designated my personality type as psychotic but I found ways to throw the shrink off the scent. I didn't offer an honest depiction of myself; I made all the answers to their questions up. They can never really get to you. The whole basis of psychological profiling is a fallacy. I'm sure they know all this, too. So what the fuck is the point? It's just a little game of show and tell whereby you tell them everything and show them nothing.

This morning, after going down the mess hall for my bacon and eggs, I was having my 20 minutes in the yard. I was standing by the wall smoking a cigarette. Even the air outside around the prison is an inescapable foul mixture of steel, disinfectant, sweat and human waste. Danny saw me and cut through the feculent stench towards me. He stood for a few moments and then leaned into me: "See that screw over there, the big fooker? Don't let that bastard get you alone. Fookin' nonce, he is. He'll fookin' slick-leg you. The scumbag should be locked up with all the other fookin' nonces in 'ere, know what I mean?"

I wasn't familiar with the prison lingo. Though I was to find out later, I had no idea what getting slick-legged was, I just nodded and changed the subject.

"Hey," I offered Danny a smoke. "I reckon I'll have a gram or two of that Whizz as soon as you can get it."

"No problem," Danny nodded slowly, looking ruminatively across the yard, staring at the guards staring at the men as he struck a match in his cupped hand, "I'll start thinking of something you can trade for it." He placed the cigarette between his lips and lit it.

No Exit

I turned and walked back here to the wing, where I'm sitting now, whittling away the time, waiting for my £5-a-week job to materialise.

WHAT'S INSIDE A GIRL

She puts on her lipstick in the rear view mirror. There's no glimmer of light reflecting in her black as black Ray Bans.

"Where to next?" she asks, lipstick poised in her hand.

"Wherever the road takes us." I gun the accelerator.

Beneath a sky brilliant with stars white as boneskulls, we drive between launderettes and service stations. On the run. Coast to coast. Forever lost in the afterbirth of countless still-born towns.

I pull over at a Motel and in the room Eve rests her warm body against mine, stroking her fingers over the tattoo on my left shoulder.

"I fucking love you," she traces her fingers over the text between the two converging guitars, "Mister Eddie C."

I nod and spark up another cigarette. "Of course you do, baby."

Eve slowly runs her hot tongue up my thigh and says: "Mmm...yeah....do it in my mouth."

I lean back on the bed, watching my cigarette smoke curl upwards.

I had picked Eve up somewhere in Death Valley. It had been sizzling hot that morning and when a summer thunderstorm punctured the simmering atmosphere, the rain evaporated upon contact with the still boiling asphalt.

I had no money left. No smokes. No drink. No drugs. And I was running out of fuel again. I was out of almost everything. But lady luck hadn't blown me a goodbye kiss just yet. I still had some good fortune left in the tank.

I skidded to a stop just past her outstretched thumb. In the door mirror I watched her slink toward the car in a pair of high heeled, red leather boots. She was wearing skin-tight battered old jeans and a leopard-skin waistcoat with nothing underneath and I was thinking *holy shit.*

She leaned inside the car and caught me with a look.

"Jesus Christ," she smiled, getting in. "Where'd y'get the Barracuda?"

I held out my palms matter-of-factly, "Some people just got it all, baby."

We'd driven for a few miles when the steering started pulling to the left and I thought I'd gotten a flat so I pulled over to the side of the road. I walked around the car but the tyres turned out to be a-o-k. I thought it was probably all the dry dust getting caught up in the wheels and the brake pads. I took a moment to stand and take in the barren desert views.

Eve got out and stood looking at the scorched, golden landscape with me. It was like being on another planet. I was standing leaning with my back against the car when Eve turned to me.

"You like girls who like to play dirty?"

"Yeah," I shrugged. "I suppose."

And right there by the side of the road, she unbuttoned my Levi's and got down on her knees.

Apart from a pack of Juicy Fruit and a loaded Smith & Wesson in her handbag, Eve didn't have anything to her name either.

"You can't sit around waiting for them to give you anythin' in this life," she said. "You gotta take what you can get."

A little further along the road we pulled over at a Shell gas station. We sat in the car for a few minutes checking out the territory. There was no sign of anything. Not that I even cared. Anything, whatever it might be, to me, would constitute being just another whitewashed day.

Eve took out the revolver and said, "Let's do it!"

Well, what else could I do? She passed the gun to me and I stuffed it in my belt and covered it over with my corduroy shirt. We walked in the place casually, hand in hand.

The cashier was a pretty peroxide blonde with just a hint of the dark roots beginning to show through. She was wearing a little old-fashioned gingham dress that was pink and white. She had bright red lipstick and she was sitting behind the counter nonchalantly filing her nails. Her name badge said Marjorie Alonso. She didn't as much as look up at us until I took out the gun and stuck it in her little Mexican face.

"Open the register, Marjorie," I told her.

She dropped the metal nail file on the floor and threw her hands over her heart. She stuttered for a moment and then said, "I can't... you... you gotta buy somethin' before I can open the drawer."

Eve tossed back her black hair and blew a bubble with her gum. "Just open the till, Strawberry Lips, or he's gonna spread that pretty face up the wall." The bubble burst with a pop. "We're not fuckin' around here, Marj. He's got one bullet in that gun and at the moment it's got your name on it."

I looked Marjorie in the eyes and cocked the hammer, "Comprende, Senorita?"

Marjorie's little hands were trembling. She fumbled about tapping at the buttons on the till – bleep bleep bleep bleep – until finally the thing kerchinged open. I reached over and shoved her out the way before grabbing all the notes and stuffing in them in my pockets.

"Oh and... hmm" Eve pointed at the cigarette cabinet behind Marjorie. "Give us three packs of Marlboro and a box of matches."

"And then I'd like you to go outside and fill up the tank," I ordered, waving her out with the gun. "Just make it all look as natural as can be, there's a good girl."

While Marjorie pumped the fuel Eve grabbed a brown grocery bag and stocked up on food supplies. I smashed the glass front of a display cabinet and took us two pairs of Ray Bans.

Just as we were exiting the store Marjorie made a dash for it.

"That stupid bitch," Eve shoved the bag of groceries into my arms and took the revolver. "We're in the middle of nowhere. Where's she think she's gonna run to?"

There was a dried-up stream running alongside the gas station. Marjorie bolted over to it and jumped in. We could still see the top of her stupid bright blonde head. Eve strolled over, her steel-tipped heels clouting the station forecourt. She stood over Marjorie with her legs spread each side of the narrow ditch, pointing the gun at the cowering Marjorie's head.

"You stupid little bitch," Eve spat. She made Marjorie sweat it for a few moments before finally lowering the gun and shoving Marjorie down onto her side with her heel. "You've been a good girl, Marjorie. Now just stay down there, real low, until you're sure we're long gone outta here. D'you get my drift?"

Marjorie covered her face with her hands and started to murmur, "This can't be real, this can't be real. It isn't happening."

"Listen," Eve shoved the cold muzzle of the gun in her face. "It's as real as it gets, Bitch. Don't make me hit you 'round the head with this hunk of metal cos' it ain't never gonna feel like a marshmallow."

"That was cool," Eve laughed when we were back in the Barracuda, gunning it along the road.

"Jesus Christ, for a minute there I thought you were gonna blow the girl's fucking brains out."

"Oh naw, I aint never gonna kill no one."

Eve counted the stash as I drove. We'd pulled $950. "I love you," she said, rubbing all the notes between her palms. "What's your name?"

"I'm Eddie Cochran, baby."

Eve laughed again, a little bit too much, still high on adrenaline. "No really, what's your fucking name?"

So I told her again – yeah, my name is Eddie Cochran. "What do you wanna see? My fucking tattoo?"

"What kinda parents would call their kid that?"

"Mine would," I answered. "They're dead now. I never really knew them."

This time Eve just looked at me dead straight and said, "Yeah? Do you wear a cobra snake for a necktie, too?"

"Nah, you've got that wrong, kid." I put one of the Marlboro's between my lips. "That was my friend, Bo Diddley who wore the necktie."

We drove until we found a roadside diner and bar called the Blue Monkey, where we played Stray Cats on the jukebox and sat at the bar drinking draught beer with Jack and Coke chasers until we were both falling off our stools. We met a guy with straggly long hair and thick, black sideburns in there who called himself Johnny Toledo.

Toledo took one look at us and said, "If you wanna little bit of fuel - you come to Johnny Toledo."

He had a battered Ford truck outside that he went wheel-spinning off in as soon we'd scored two hundred dollars of H off him. He left so fast I thought we'd been ripped off but it turned out to be pretty good shit. After we left the Blue Monkey Eve and I booked a room at the 49er Motel just a little further along from the bar. The room was luxury compared to the places I'd been squatting down in the last few weeks. It was crisp and clean and had a TV and CD player. By this time it was dark and the motel's neon sign outside was lit up, flashing. It flashed through the thin yellow curtains in our room alternating the bare walls blue and red, blue and red.

Eve carried her works with her in a little leather zip up case that she kept in her handbag. We each shot up the H, sharing Eve's syringe. In sharing blood, we became bonded to each other. In seconds I felt the H seep deep into my bones.

We drifted like this for what seemed like hours. Tiny ions in the air detonated and sparked, all known geometry failed. The world slid out of view. For those few hours we were drifting, immersed in a sea of hot honey, exempt from the anguish of living.

Eve peeled off that tight leopard-skin waistcoat. She had big firm tits with dark red nipples. I lay back on the bed toying with the revolver, spinning the silver barrel round and round, creating shimmering reflections up the wall. I was just trying to act cool, as if I'd seen a million other girls like Eve before. But I hadn't; I thought she was fucking beautiful.

The first time I did H it made me feel like I'd been amongst the walking dead all my life and had only then been made to realise it. The laws of physics cease and the normal distinctions we make in everyday life become defunct. When you see the world without illusions you see it's not a pretty place. Heroin provides sanctuary and you never want to return to the life you knew before. Like an impassioned Christian, you become born again. Overwhelmed by the holy spirit inside you.

And there was no antidote. Eve was my new love, a new drug in my system. She still had on her thigh-hugging faded jeans and high-heel red leather boots. I made her take everything off – everything except the shiny, patent leather knee-length boots. She stood with her hands on her hips with one knee resting on the bed. Her pussy was shaved, exposing labia the colour of a dark rose.

Looking down at me with her black, silky hair hanging over her shoulders, she drawled: "You wanna know what's inside a girl?"

I placed the Smith & Wesson on the bedside table, wrapped my arm tightly around her waist.

"Yeah, come here, you little fucking bitch."

As she squealed and I dragged her down on the bed with me, the light became brighter and brighter and the world suddenly stopped turning on its axis, throwing the motel room into a tailspin of whirling white heat.

"Come on, baby," I tell Eve. "We've got to get out of here."

I fetch out my map and study it. "We're gonna get on the 15, drive down to San Diego and then escape to Mexico."

She finishes touching-up her lipstick and tosses the little tube back in her bag as I punch the accelerator.

Between gas stations and motels. Expressway lights slither across her Ray Ban lenses. Veins become crystalline. We are in love and the rest of the world peels away like dead paint.

What's Inside A Girl

THE RAG AND BONE MAN

The neighbour's dog was whining in the night again. Its mournful dog-song echoed around the houses. It woke Joe Fuegi up. He hadn't made it into bed. He'd been drunk again, on his own in the house, talking to himself, crashing over the coffee table, falling over chairs. Throughout the evening he'd consumed a whole bottle of Johnny Walker Red Label in front of the TV and when he woke up the TV channel was on close-down for the night; the plain blue screen glowed, bathing the room in a cold, icy hue. Joe awoke to find himself sitting up in the chair, still in his clothes, with his head slumped forward on his chest. *Aooowwwwoooo. Aooowwwwoooo.* The dog wouldn't shut up. And it was 3 a.m. Joe's hand had tipped forwards with the tumbler in it and spilled the last drop of whisky on his empty trouser leg.

Joe Fuegi had been born in Bloxwich Maternity Home with his left leg missing from the knee down. For the rest of his life he'd had to wear a prosthetic limb. The deformed leg ended in a hard, bony stump instead of a knee joint, and the stump had to be inserted into a

The Rag and Bone Man

rubber cup in the leg. A lace-up leather harness then had to be strapped around his thigh to hold then hinged lower limb in place. After wearing the leg for hours on end it was a relief to take it off in the evenings. It was a heavy chunk of machinery to wear all day, removing it was the same feeling as relieving the jaw of an aching tooth and Joe frequently massaged lanolin into the sore, rough skin that formed on the malformed limb.

    He always propped the leg against the side of his chair as he sat and drank and watched TV. He liked the game shows. It bought a lump to his throat to see people win the big, life-changing prizes. Well, some of the people anyway. He grabbed his metal limb, rolled up his trouser leg and strapped it on. He went into the kitchen and chopped some liver into strips and put it in the dog's plastic dish. It was a cold, star spangled night out there and he didn't like the way the neighbours abandoned the poor dog outside all night. Their cluttered yard backed onto his and there was a loose vertical slat in the fence. He went out and swung it aside. The mad white Jack Russell terrier would always come tearing through, licking Joe's hands.

    Just as Joe so often did, he carried the excited hound inside and fed it the chopped liver treats. He thought he'd heard the neighbours calling the dog Freddy but Joe named it Adolf because it had a tiny black mark like a moustache beneath its nose. After Adolf had finished eating Joe lay down on the sofa and the dog jumped up and lay next to him, nestling its hard, muscular little Jack Russell body tight and warm against Joe's chest. He slept off the drink until about

The Rag and Bone Man

8 am. Then he carried Adolf back outside and slipped him back through the fence.

The paperboy had already stuffed the early morning edition of the Express & Star through the letterbox. After sitting and briefly leafing through a few pages of all the parochial bullshit Joe put on his crumpled overcoat and headed out for breakfast. He got in the battered Ford pick-up truck and motored into town. He parked on Smallbrook Queensway outside the music shop and walked around the corner to the Sunny Day Café. It was a cheap but clean enough place on Hurst Street with little blue table cloths and nets up the windows, owned by a short, fat Italian man called Sergio.

Joe ordered his usual bacon, sausage and eggs with fried bread. Sergio's English was shit; he just nodded and wiped down his hands on his grease-stained apron. While Sergio stood frying the food at the cooker Joe sat and waited at one of blue tableclothed tables situated right in the middle of the room.

A little girl about five years old walked over and stood staring at him. She was a sickly looking child, extremely thin and her hair was falling out in clumps. Her skin had a yellow hue to it and one of her eyes appeared to be clouded over. She was beautiful. It was heart-wrenching to look at her. Childhood cancer, Joe reckoned, feeling tears well up in his eyes. A feeling of awfulness instilled itself in Joe's chest. He could only describe it as a sense of helplessness, and a kind of fear, though he had no idea why.

"What's wrong with your face?" the little girl asked.

"It's called a tumour," Joe told her. "But I'm okay. It just looks funny. It's called a benign tumour." He reached up and touched the small growth, about the size of a cherry tomato that hung from the right side of his face.

"I'm poorly, too," the girl nodded. "And the other children at school are okay but sometimes their mommies and daddies tell them to stay away from me."

Joe felt as if the tears were going to break into a full blown river. She looked so vulnerable he wanted to wrap her up in cotton wool. He reached out and stroked her face. "That's because in this world people can be truly vile. But they can't change... it's just the way they are. When they don't understand something they act stupid. If you try and keep that in mind it makes them a little bit easier to deal with."

"My name's Mathilda," the little girl smiled, stepping closer towards him. She had on a little Tartan skirt and fluffy pink sweater. "What's yours?"

"Joe."

"I like you, Joe."

"I like you, too." Joe smiled, swallowing a lump in his throat, gently reaching out and playfully pinching her tiny nose.

The girl's mother, a dark haired woman with a hardened, strained face, came over from her corner table and without even acknowledging Joe, picked the girl up and carried her away. She was a vastly overweight woman, the kind who broke beds, not hearts. Over her mother's shoulder Mathilda looked back and waved.

"People really stink!" Joe added, under his breath. Just what in the name of God did life do to the fuckers to make them the way they are?

He ate his breakfast and swilled it down with a mug of Sergio's strong, orange coloured tea. He paid the bill and said goodbye to Mathilda with a little child-like waggle of his fingers. The girl's fat slob of a mother didn't even look up. She sat staring miserably into her now empty, stained tea cup.

Loitering outside the café there was some teenage kid wearing a woolly hat and duffel coat. "Got any spare change?" he begged, with a foul kind of patronising stoop.

"No, I'm sorry, I haven't," Joe acknowledged without breaking step.

"Yeah, jog on, bro', look after yourself. Look after number one!" the kid said, breathing into his hands and stamping his feet, pitifully making out it was colder than it actually was. He was so transparently playing the victim Joe would never have given him anything. The world was so annoyingly awash with such fucking victims these days. Most of them didn't know they were born and in actuality, had very little they should be whimpering and wetting their pants about. Like this cunt. Absolutely nothing stopping him from pulling himself up by his bootstraps.

"Son," Joe stopped walking and held out his palms. "I like whisky. No one's gonna give me it for nothing... So that means I gotta work. You want money for whatever you want it for, then you gotta work for it."

The Rag and Bone Man

It was Saturday; market day. And on market days Joe always got his vegetables from Dave. Dave the Rave, everyone called him, on account of his excessive drug binges in the dance clubs around town. Joe was too old for all that shit now, but he knew about Dave. Dave was just one of those characters every man and his dog knew. Dave was full of shit though. Personally, Joe jokingly referred to Dave the Rave as Baron Bullshit. Dave owned and ran the fruit and veg stall on the market in St. Martin's Square.

Joe walked towards the market back along Smallbrook Queensway, past where he'd parked the Ford, when he realised he desperately needed to drop some bombs. He'd have to use the queers' toilets near the underpass by the Rotunda. The Cottages, all the gays called them. Now, he didn't have anything against homos. Live and let live was Joe's motto. But he did have something against the kind of people that frequented the Cottages. Whatever one's persuasion they could not much be considered savoury characters. They were amongst the lowest echelons of society. He considered walking back to the Café but he might not make it after last night's chicken bhuna. So he limped into one of the disgusting cubicles in the Cottages and sat down. An amalgamation of rancid smells grabbed you in the stomach and twisted your insides as soon as you walked in the place. It stank like something had died in there and then a dozen of them had shot their bolt all over the corpse.

There was a hole crudely hacked into the dividing partition between him and the next cubicle. The glory hole. Joe hastily plugged it up with a good handful of the cheap toilet tissue that'd been unravelled all over the floor. Across the inside of his cubicle door some two-bit philosopher had scrawled in electric blue marker pen: 'when I die bury me upside down so the world can kiss my ass.' As he sat on the toilet waiting for his bomb doors to open the tissue was suddenly poked out of the hole from the other side by an erect penis. It was a curved, ruddy appendage with a grotesque smeg-encrusted head and, along with a matted knot of thick, black pubic hair; it protruded through the hole and just hung there waiting. Joe leaned away from the thing and looked around for a bog-brush or whatever else to give it a good, hard smack with but there was nothing at hand. Then an eager, breathy voice from the other side of the partition demanded, "Suck it and see!"

"I'm going to give you one chance – and one chance only – to get that outta my face, *now*!" Joe warned, trying as hard as he could to inject a touch of cautionary venom into his words. There was no reply. Looking up towards the open top of the cubicle Joe shouted over, "Let me put it another way, you betta put that back in your trousers or I'll cut it off and shove it down your throat, you understand me, Sunshine?"

"Come onnnnn... you know you want to... what else are you here for? *Suck it!* See what happens."

"I'm in here to have a shit, pal. Bit of a curry last night, know what I mean?" Joe waited, still wanting to give the dirty bastard a chance to reconsider. But instead, whoever was the other side persisted. "Loll-ee-pop, loll-eeeee-pop," he started singing the old Chordettes song and bouncing his cock up and down. "Ooooh lolly lolly lolly lolly pop-a-loll-eeee-pop."

Joe hurriedly finished what he was doing, pulled up his trousers, flushed, and went around to the next cubicle. He shouldered the door open, sending splintered shards of wood spinning from the broken bolt. He grabbed the guy under the chin, shoving him hard against the shit and blood-smeared wall, squeezing the sides of his face so that his lips bunched up like a fish. "*I'll* fucking lollipop you," Joe spat, pulling his Stanley knife out his pocket and pressing it against the guy's throat.

It was then Joe realised this was just some urchin of a skinny kid, maybe nineteen or twenty. He let go of him and watched him slump down on the toilet, holding his finger-bruised throat.

"Jesus Christ," the kid coughed. "You've got a serious problem, man." His skin was youthful and as yet unblemished by life. He looked like he didn't even shave properly yet.

"I'm the one with the problem?" Joe waved a hand around the room. "There's shit smeared up the walls in this place for God's sake. Son, what the fuck are you doing in here? You're just a young man. Go and find yourself a proper boyfriend if that's what you want. Get out and do something with your life."

Joe retracted the blade and returned the cutting tool to his pocket. "Yeah," he laughed as he turned and walked out of the stinking cesspit, shaking his head. "It's me. I'm all that's wrong with the world."

Joe Fuegi was fifty-two years old. When he was eighteen, near enough the same age as that kid, his parents were killed in a London tube train crash when the train slammed into the end of a dead-end tunnel at Moorgate. Joe had inherited his father's scrap yard in Yardley. That's right; he was a rag 'n' bone man. It was a title he liked the sound of. He'd always expected that some director would make a horror film called *The Rag 'n' Bone Man* someday. It sounded rightly terrifying. The rag 'n' bone man sounded like someone who dabbled in black magic, someone who summoned the devil. The rag 'n' bone man is the face you see peering in through bleak farmhouse windows on lightning spliced nights. The rag n bone man comes for you in the night, meting out his own twisted idea of justice.

He'd lived and worked the scrapyard all his life. His parents had been in the first car. The investigation report said the thirty-foot carriage was completely crushed by the impact, concertinaed down to just about two feet. No one travelling in it stood a chance. That was in 1975 and he was listening to the Loaded album by The Velvet Underground when he got the news. There was no other family to speak of and Joe had pretty much been alone since that moment when the policeman turned up at the door carrying his helmet under his arm and pseudo-solemnly dropped the bombshell.

There's a song on the Loaded album called Train Round the Bend. It was playing at the solitary moment Joe closed the door and found himself alone in the world for the first time. The realisation had run him through like a rapier. He shivered even now as he recalled the incisive cacophony of silence that pervaded the house immediately after hearing. No one could ever adequately describe in words the moment your blood just freezes in your veins, leaving you numb. You don't start feeling the pain until days later when your blood vessels begin to thaw. One thing the experience taught Joe was that life is too short to deny someone their own chosen pleasures in life.

Ever since he was a kid Joe collected tin soldiers. He used to play with them. Now he had thousands of them standing in orderly platoons in glass display cabinets in his living room. Napoleonic and First World War mainly, but also a few American Civil War. He liked the way they were devoid of a soul. They were hollow and couldn't be hurt. Even when the paint began to chip away from their faces and their uniforms they didn't feel anything inside. Joe had wished he was like that. But he wasn't.

Having been born without his left leg he was set apart from everyone else. Children can be so accommodating in their curiosity but people in general could be cruel and that's why he'd experienced an immediate rapport with the little girl in the café. He understood her, empathised with how isolated others made her feel. But it wasn't that, exactly, that had gotten to him. It was just the way most other people didn't think about anything too deeply. They didn't feel or appreciate anything. They were like his collection of tin soldiers: like Joe sometimes wanted to be. But being the way he was had above all instilled in him more empathy for the human condition than most other people would ever understand. Most of them would go to their graves in utter ignorance.

Joe watched people. As a child he always felt the inner pain of being the one on the outside looking in. And that sensitivity to the world around him had left him with scars inside. He was painfully aware that that's how Mathilda would be feeling right now and there was nothing he or anyone else could do for her. Involvement with other people was all too often like swallowing broken glass, it tore him up inside. But he'd also learned that in life it was simply the force of your will against the world. It has been said that only the tough survive. But Joe reckoned that wasn't entirely correct. He was tough enough alright. Life had made him that way; life had turned his heart to stone. But being tough was no defence against the relentless march of the hollow men. If you had a heart the world would drive a nail right through it. Even a heart of stone can be shattered with a single sledge-hammer blow. And Joe's had been shattered. He just didn't let anyone see it. He didn't let anyone get too close.

He'd always been glad he'd never had any whining, whinging children. Apart from the fact that kids fuck up your life, it was because he didn't want to be disappointed in them. But as he'd aged he realised that was just a defence mechanism. The truth was that he always thought it would be him who disappointed them as a father. He feared intimacy with other human beings. This was a part of himself he'd simply learned to accept. It is said that you should always look at the state of a man's shoes. Joe always made sure he checked the backs of them as well because people are always concealing something unsavoury beneath the polished and glossy front they present to the world around them. It's all just enamel covering the gaping cracks in the hearts of men.

When Joe got to Dave the Rave's market stall Dave was standing beneath the striped canopy of another trader's stall with his hands thrust into the money bag attached to the waistband at the front of his faded jeans, loudly telling the other stall-holder one of his tales. Joe often secretly referred to these stories as The Bullshit Chronicles. He was thinking of writing a book of The Bullshit Chronicles. Joe wasn't sure if anyone else had noticed how Dave was always so full of shit. As he got closer Joe only caught the tail-end of whatever un-funny bullshit story Dave was spouting...

"... So the coppers raided the place. Everybody chucking their gear on the floor, you know? But there's me, handful of Doves... ha ha ha ha ha ha..." Dave threw a cupped hand to his mouth in demonstration. "Swallowed the fuckin' lot like that... Ha ha ha ha."

Dave's shaved head had turned purple from laughter. He slapped the other stall-holder on the back, doubled over in hysterics.

He formed a circle with his two hands, "Yeah, the fucking things were the size of biscuits, man, I swear. I was off my fucking trolley the rest of the night, slumped up the corner, chewing me face off, I was. Only woke up to tell one of the coppers to fuck off."

Both men rocked around with laughter and then Dave spotted Joe and came bounding over to where Joe was stood waiting. "Joe, my man, so what you know?" he shouted, punching Joe on the top of his arm.

"Erm... not much. I've seen nothing, I've heard nothing, and I know nothing, Dave. 'Bout you?"

Baron Bullshit picked up a brown paper bag and started filling it with Joe's usual order. "Ah, not much," he shook his head emphatically. "Yeah, I'm hearin' ya. Same all over, man!" he agreed in his usual disinterested tone, staring out into the bustling crowds of shoppers as he carelessly tossed the items into the bag.

Judging by the yellowy eyes and sallow complexion Dave had obviously been out raving again the last few nights. The anaemic skin tone suggested the few morsels of calcium and iron that might have once resided in his body had been sucked out of the kid. Joe guessed Dave must have been about twenty-seven. Joe had qualified quite some time ago that Dave was something of a cretin; he didn't have too much time for druggies but that wasn't the reason he didn't like Dave very much. He was just a cunt.

Something else Joe had often noticed was a very faint, almost imperceptible, pissy smell about Dave. It wafted in the vicinity around him, arriving a few seconds before his physical presence like a forewarning. Joe wasn't entirely sure what could be causing it but it was most disconcerting, as if there was something putrid emanating from the very core of the man's being.

"Hey Dave," Joe pointed. "Drop me some of those asparagus spears in, I'm making a risotto tonight."

"WOOAH RISOTTO-LOTTO!" Baron Bullshit flung the wrap of asparagus spears high in the air and caught them in the brown bag like a fielder catching a cricket ball. He folded over the top of the bag and presented it to Joe. "Three-fifty-eight," he said, with a fake cheerful wink of his horrid waxy eye. It dawned on Joe what a slippery little sperm stain Baron Bullshit truly was. He considered the possibility of not shopping at Dave's grubby little market stall again. He was fucked if he knew why he'd been coming there in the first place.

Dave stretched out his potato-soiled palm and Joe counted out the exact money in small change, tucked the bag under his arm and waved, "See you, Dave."

"Not if I see you first," the predictable twat clicked his tongue and made as if he was shooting a gun at Joe with his two fingers. He did that every single time. Fucking cretin.

On the way back to his truck Joe stopped at the butcher's stall and bought some fresh liver for little Adolf. Simply by their purity of existence Joe felt more for animals than he did for most people. And with little Adolf he especially felt some sense of friendship. Both he and the dog were, he supposed, two of life's abandoned outcasts in one way or another.

Joe placed his bags of shopping on the passenger seat. He was looking forward to tonight's risotto for two. He had his girlfriend coming round tonight. Yeah, when all was said and done old Joe Fuegi was one of life's good eggs, even though he said so himself. He'd somewhat landed on his feet with Connie. She was pretty with long red hair, twenty years younger than Joe and her skin was golden and flawless as sun-bleached sands. With most of her kin locked up in mental institutions Connie had grown up in children's homes and, like Joe, was a little fucked up in the head. She was kind of crazy herself and Joe liked that about her.

Connie was destined to pursue happiness all the days of her life and never truly find it. She'd always looked in the wrong places. She drifted around, searched the faces of strangers in the all night cafés and motorway service stations, eventually finding her way to Joe. He didn't know much, he was just an old dog these days. But he did know there was at least some kind of affinity between them, so who knows...

"Maybe this will last between us," Joe said tentatively as they lazed in bed smoking cigarettes one Sunday morning.

"Nothing lasts," Connie told him somewhat severely. "Sometimes we think life is going so well but it's only a matter of time. We're all only ever sucking the candy-coating off a bitter pill."

It was certainly unusual to meet women at seedy, back-street porn cinemas where the stench of come and disinfectant welds together and hangs heavy in the murky air, a nauseating mixture that sticks in your nostrils. But Joe and Connie had indeed met a couple of years before in the Sunset Cinema Club on Hinckley Street during a showing of Garage Girls on one of the eighties classics nights. Connie watched him masturbate on the back row before kneeling between his legs and letting him finish in her soft, wet, coaxing mouth. They started seeing each other frequently after that.

"All I ever wanted," she said. "Was someone to love. And not be just two broken halves, relying on each other to make up one broken whole. But I guess we fucked up there!"

So Connie became Joe's companion. And she always wanted to be fucked to within an inch of her life. Joe was happy enough with that for now, happy about this slice of beauty that had drifted randomly into his life like a butterfly in the wind.

Smiling, he twisted the tea-spoon handle wedged in the ignition and fired the old rust-bucket up. The sun had come out now and he turned on the radio in time to hear *Alright Now* by Free just kicking in at that exact moment. Joe cranked the volume high as it would go, rammed the auto box into D and threaded the vehicle into a gap in the flow of frantic late morning traffic.

WOMAN

I stayed propping up the bar until after closing time. I made my way back shitfaced to The Katz bed and breakfast, zigzagging through the midweek town after all the clubs and bars had closed. I didn't even know if I was drunk any more or whether, like everything else in my life, it was just an act. The aftermath of a rainstorm tinged with bright yellow street lights glistened as it rushed along the gutters. As far as I was concerned the torrent could easily have been the very lifeblood of every damned soul that resided in this toe-rag of a town. Everybody's blood pissing away down the stinking sewers. A passing car blasting out David Bowie's *Golden Years* shattered the relative silence.

1975, and I am just a kid again. I'm sitting on a boulder on Morecambe beach. The great thundering sea is spectacular, rumbling in and dramatically smashing against the rocks. The immense cacophony is an exhilarating symphony. The beaches there were wild and rugged in those days, before the council moved in and bulldozed the whole thing, flattened it all off, made it all nice and featureless for the soulless modern tourist.

When I made it back to the b+b, Jim Katz the owner was still milling about the reception area. Even at this late hour pretending he was doing some of his chores. He had a yellow duster in one hand and a spray-bottle of surface cleaner in the other. I presumed this was all for show since I'd never seen him actually using the stuff in his filthy hovel. Katz had a small face with intense, beady eyes, the skin stretched too tight and the lips hard and rigid. He rather had the appearance of a snake. It's true to say his creator had not been generous to him in the looks department. To top it all off his bald patch was coming along splendidly by the day.

Katz and I didn't exchange any pleasantries as I staggered across the reception area to the stairs. He looked to be clean shaven... except that I thought I detected a slight dark shadow appearing between his nose and top lip. On the landing I ran into Angela who was returning from the bathroom. I was struggling like an imbecile to get the key in my door.

The fact was I'd been acting all my life, not because I was intentionally pretending to be someone else but because I've never known who I am. They did tests. They wired me up to machines and came to the conclusion I am borderline schizoid. Truth be told, I have all manner of psychological glitches.

"That landlord makes me puke," Angela pulled a face, nodding back towards the stairs. "The creepy fucker."

"Yeah, the creepy bastard," I agreed. "Did you notice he's growing a moustache?"

"Dear God," she laughed.

I eventually managed to wangle my way through the door. I caught my pocket on the door handle as I fell in. I heard Angela laugh at my trousers tearing open as I staggered all the way across the room, gambolled onto the bed and flopped out in all my clothes, out cold for the night; the crotch of my trousers all torn open and one leg half ripped off. And when I woke up at approaching noon the next day, I'd pissed the bed.

That was how I first met Angela. She was staying in a room just down the hall. I noticed there was something intensely sad about her. I couldn't put my finger on what it was exactly. A sad kind of air. She subsequently told me it all started with a simple infection from using dirty needles.

"You can still fuck me, I still need to know that I'm desirable as a woman," she said. "You can fuck me up the ass, you can fuck me between my thighs, and you can fuck me in the mouth. I'll be your perfect little blue-eyed fuck-doll, I'll let you tie me down and use me as a sex object and I won't ever complain or answer back. I'll be yours alone and I'll be everything and anything you ever dreamed of."

So when we fucked the only difference from the accepted norm was just that it was up her ass, that's all. It became our norm. And looking down at her beautiful face, her tousled long, blonde hair fanned out over the pillow, it made entirely no difference to me. I had fallen hopelessly in love with her. She had completely devoured me. Angela looked like a perfect work of sculpted bone china. Everything I ever thought beautiful in the world had, in Angela, reached a single point of infinity. My erotic interest was with her mind. It was for the first time in my life that I'd experienced that kind of desire. In winter I wanted to wrap her up and keep her safe and warm. I wanted to be her suit of armour.

"You think that's what I need, to be rescued?" She asked me whimsically, sucking her finger as if it was a lollipop.

"Maybe you don't. But it's what I need," I said. "I always needed someone to rescue. Someone who needs me."

Angela Valentine had no tits and no vagina. At the age of twenty-seven she had the body of an innocent little girl. The infection she told me about had resulted in her having a mastectomy followed by a full vulvectomy after she'd shot up in the groin. From her armpits to where her breasts should be, there were just two thin, long scars. But they were able to save her nipples which had been somehow re-attached to her flat chest and in which she had retained some sensitivity. One of her remaining pleasures was having them licked and sucked.

Down below there was nothing. She was smooth shaved and there was a barely visible scar and just a tiny little pee-hole that she enjoyed having caressed but was too small to penetrate.

All the scars were almost transparent, everything knitted back together so neatly and carefully. The doctors had done a tidy job of making her look like a little doll. It reminded me of the thrill I used to feel as a young kid inquisitively looking up the skirts of my cousin's toy dolls, attempting to uncover the mystery of what the hell women had that was different to me. I think that's what I found so oddly titillating about Angela. She was my toy doll made flesh; mentally regressing me to that place in childhood, satisfying my unfulfilled boyish desires and curiosities.

"I'm clean now," she'd blurted out. "But I was shooting up. I haven't touched the stuff in five years now. But it's fucked me up in ways you can't begin to imagine."

She started undressing and said: "I want to show you."

"You don't have to do all this," I remember assuring her, taking her hand in mine.

"No, it's easier for me this way. I have to get this over with. Then it's all out in the open between us."

I later came to believe she'd planned her seduction as if she could read some inherent facet of my being. She wouldn't have done it if she hadn't have been sure. She stood before me in nothing but a black fishnet body-stocking. Her dark red nipples protruded through the criss-cross holes. I pulled her down onto the bed, tore the body-stocking open at the crotch and fucked her hard in the ass, running my hands over her svelte body. My own little doll to play with. And she loved it as much as I did. She wilted in my arms like a flower in the breeze.

"Oh my god," she said. Her blue eyes glinted in the half-light. "That was amazing. I needed to know I could still feel something. Something physical."

Woman

Angela kissed me on the mouth and said, "I'll let you keep me in a wooden trunk at the bottom of your bed and only fetch me out whenever you want to do that to me again and again."

Something profound happened one day a month later when we walked into town. In the window of a junk shop just off the high street there was an old, tatty jester marionette hanging by its strings. It peered out at the town with its twisted grin, a wooden tear carved into his painted lime-wood face trickled sadly down his cheek. I'd seen that dead behind the eyes look in men before. It was a wise face; he knew that when all is said and done, this fucking life was nothing more than flowers in the fist of a corpse.

There was a hand-written sign tacked to his red and green coat that said: MAKE ME AN OFFER.

I turned to Angela and said, "We've gotta get out of this shit-hole of a town. Let's go away somewhere together."

"Yes! But I don't care about the price," she nodded happily, linking her arm tightly in mine. "We can't just leave *him* behind."

DISINTERGRATION

It was all nothing but human dust. Wasted lives that never amounted to anything. There were no words of lamentation spilling from Frank's lips. What did it matter, ultimately? In the grand scheme of things most human lives were no more important than ants. He turned away from the funeral procession rolling its way along Moseley high street towards the church, the coffins in the back of the hearses draped in Union Jacks and military regalia. Frank continued walking past the lines of sombre onlookers lining the pavements until he reached the corner and flung open the heavy, smoked glass door of The Fighting Cocks. He went in and sat down on a stool at the bar. An old Fleetwood Mac song was playing quietly in the background.

A day off work at least for employee number 714967. Yesterday at work on the production line he raised his hand, indicating to his line manager that he wanted to go for a piss. You had to raise your hand when you wanted the can, so that a contingency plan could be effected in order to not slow down the production line. It was right hand for toilet leave, left hand for some other problem. In the designated area he removed his white paper suit and hair net. It was all marked down in the manager's book. As he walked out into the corridor and down the long staircase with its black plastic banister and metal rails a recorded voice on the in-house radio that constantly echoed throughout the distribution centre told him:

"WE TAKE PRIDE IN WHAT WE DO. EVERY HOUR OF EVERY DAY WE PUT OUR CUSTOMERS FIRST!"

After he'd taken his slash the urinal flushed automatically and an electronic voice gently reminded him: "now please wash your hands." A printed sign taped on the mirrors above the ceramic basins read, STOP SPITTING AND BLOWING YOUR NOSES IN THE WASH BASINS – REMEMBER IT IS ONE OF YOUR COLLEAGUES THAT HAS TO CLEAN IT UP!

He squeezed one of his nostrils and with all his might blew a big green glob into the sink. Have some of that, you bastards, he laughed to himself. As he trudged back up the stairs. Blondie's Atomic was interspersed with the serene female monotone issuing more brainwashing dogma:

"WE AIM FOR 100% CUSTOMER SATISFACTION. THAT'S WHAT MAKES NUMBER ONE FOR PLASTIC CARTONS BY CUSTOMERS ALL AROUND THE WORLD."

The voice was calm and methodical, with a hypnotic timbre and rhythm to it. Gently coaxing coaxing coaxing.

Disintegration

"WHAT IS THE MEANING OF SUCCESS? OUR SUCCESS IS ACHIEVED THROUGH SERVICE TO OTHERS, EVERY DAY IN EVERY WAY."

Always the same incessant brainwashing bullshit. In the end you couldn't get it out of your brain, day or night. Jesus H. Christ, he'd love to smash the speakers. He thought about going around and knocking four inch nails right into the centres of the speaker cones. They'd never spot it. It'd take 'em ages to work out what had gone wrong there. On the wall there was a brightly decorated performance chart entitled OUR TEAM WHEEL OF FORTUNE. It mapped out a long line starting from zero in the bottom left hand corner of the graph, forming a steep upward sweep and peeking at a 94% success rate pinnacle. 714967 looked over his shoulder along the deserted corridor, took out a black marker pen from his breast pocket and continued the line into a jagged, disastrous plummet right the way back down to 16%.

Through the window he saw one of his fellow workers, a curly haired man he'd never seen before, sitting on the bench in green overalls having a cigarette outside in the neatly manicured garden. Their eyes met briefly through the glass as the man looked up at the window and they both nodded acknowledgment, both bearing the same look of utter, soul- crushed resignation that everybody else in the place possessed. Maybe that was the poor bastard whose time would be spent cleaning phlegm out the sinks? Frank felt a twinge of guilt about that now.

Disintegration

Frank didn't like Colin, the barman in the Fighting Cocks. Whenever he spoke it was as if his mouth was a separate entity to his true sensibilities. He just said whatever he thought might sound the most agreeable; so whenever a conversation sparked up anything that tripped from his tongue never sounded authentic to Frank. Colin was something of a chameleon and Frank didn't trust people who don't talk straight.

It was Colin's lunch time shift and when Frank walked in he was sitting down hunched over the newspaper doing the crossword. He'd looked up from under his brow as Frank swung the door open. Halfheartedly he tossed his ballpoint pen onto the bar and sauntered over to the fridge and uncapped Frank his usual bottle of Miller. Frank unbuttoned his black pea coat and leaned with his elbows on the bar. He jerked his head back towards the doors. "This malarkey going on outside," he said, shaking his head. "I don't get it."

"Well, it was a bad thing, you know, a community thing." Colin said. "It affects everyone. We all feel it in our guts." He tapped a fist to his stomach.

Colin felt not a thing, Frank thought. "Yeah, sure. Everyone feels it in their guts, 'Course they do," Frank nodded with a grin, bottle to his lips. "Why aren't *you* out there showing your respects then?"

"What, you don't feel anything?" Colin asked, inattentively straightening the drip trays set out along the bar as he walked back to

Disintegration

his newspaper at the far end. "Look at this place," Colin waved a hand at the empty room. "Everyone's at the memorial."

"Well, as a matter of fact I don't buy into it." Frank raised a toast with his bottle and took a sip from it.

The funeral procession was for a group of local soldiers killed in Afghanistan. There were five from the Staffordshire regiment; killed by a roadside bomb.

"Some of those soldiers are little more than kids, Frank. Nineteen years old, some of 'em. It's an occasion to put aside personal politics. Now I know why everyone calls you Frank the Wanker!"

Frank shrugged, dismissively. Colin peered back down at his crossword, "Thirsty bishop might put Pepsi-Cola in the chalice. Nine letters?" Colin scratched his curly head with his pen, frowning intensely. Colin was such a little cunt, with his bleeding heart pretensions and that orange, loose-knit hippie sweater hanging nearly down to his knees. Frank was fucked if he'd have him behind any bar of his. He was also interested in all these ecology issues, animal rights, human rights; anything, in fact, that was going. Didn't eat meat or wear leather shoes and all that kind of shit. The gangly string of piss. He espoused the merits of any flavour of the month pc issues he thought made him look like a right-on guy. Frank seemed to remember he'd heard Colin referring to himself as a humanitarian. Wah wah wah wah, every time he spoke it was like listening to a fucking parrot. He even had beady eyes like one. Frank wondered whether a chameleon's skin was slimy. Colin's upper lip and brow were always sweating. A few years ago Colin had gotten himself done. Some woman had accused him of sexual harassment in the street. Frank didn't know all the ins and outs but to this day Colin had always protested he was only down there tying his shoe laces. "Yeah, right!" Frank laughed into his bottle.

"Excuse me?" Colin looked puzzled.

"Oh... nothing, just thinking out loud... talking to myself."

Frank pulled out a softpack of Marlboro's from his jeans pocket, flicked away a long strand of grey hair that had fallen across his face and put one in his mouth. He paused with the burning match lingering near the tip of the cigarette while he pondered for a moment. "Episcopal!" Frank clicked his fingers. He ignited the cigarette, shook the match in the air and waved away the dead smoke hanging around his head.

"Arrgh!" Colin thumped the bar and scribbled Episcopal in the crossword puzzle.

Frank stayed drinking at the bar the rest of the afternoon and into the evening. He laid off the bottles of Miller at about 7pm and hit the double Jameson's. Later on there was some kind of scuffle in the room. A table went over. Glasses shattered. There was a lot of shouting. One of the globe lights that hung down quite low over the bar crashed onto the floor when someone's head hit it. Everything was a blur. Frank remembered the moon appeared unusually bright

Disintegration

as he staggered home back up the high street. But he didn't actually remember *getting* home and into bed.

People in this life didn't want the truth. Everything has to be glossed over for them. Colin the barman wasn't the only example. Think of it. On toilet roll wrappers it will say something along the lines of 'extra thick – for added comfort.' It never actually spells it out: 'extra thick – so your fingers won't go through!' Frank didn't understand the hoi polloi's resistance to truth.

It was Sunday and Frank did his usual trip to the supermarket. He added the four-pack of shit roll to the shopping already in his basket as he ambled aimlessly about the aisles with these idle, meaningless thoughts going around in his head. He only ever bought food for that day and the next. He usually bought impulsively: things he didn't even need. He was always unable to plan ahead. He often bought a lot of frozen foods – and then used it the very same day.

At the checkout Frank watched the young girl robotically bleep his stuff over the scanner. She didn't smile, say hello or goodbye, or allow her gaze to meet his. She just ploughed through the items on the conveyor belt. Her sullen countenance was because the dreariness of her days spent doing the job had destroyed her soul. Her name badge said Kelly. She was trim and pretty with her blonde hair tied up in pig-tails and as Kelly packed the carrier bag with his goods Frank wondered if she had anything on other than her

Disintegration

underwear beneath the light blue work smock. He imagined her nipples, red as strawberries.

It was a murky world Frank had been living in. In the late eighties he was the vocalist in an indie trio called Sideshow Fatman. They were quite big in their heyday. They'd gigged up and down the country. Sideshow Fatman were amongst the first bands signed to the super-cool Sarah Records label and they released a single, *Set It on Fire*, and one album entitled *Generation Nihilists*. But Frank was 45 now. He was like a derelict house; populated only by the ghosts of its past. He was burned out on drugs and booze. With his leathery face most people said he looked older than his years. Admittedly, Frank *felt* weary. A lot of clued up people in the industry thought the band could have *really* hit the big time and blamed Frank Jackson for its subsequent implosion. According to an article in the NME he'd launched himself like a missile into the rock star lifestyle prematurely, and in doing so had dragged the rest of the band down with him. And, in truth, they were right. He'd fucked it all up for everyone.

What turned out to be Frank's last gig was to have been at Glasgow Barrowlands, playing support for The Wedding Present. Sarah records had provided a rider. Frank couldn't believe it and started banging back cans of Redstripe in the back of the bus on the way up. He lazed around in his sleeping bag as he drank, pissing the other guys - Jim and Dominic - off. Eventually he passed out drunk

Disintegration

with a burning Marlboro between his fingers. It resulted in the band and a couple of roadies being left standing on the hard shoulder waiting for the fire brigade with the bus and all their gear inside it burning to a cinder. Ironically that was on the fifth of November, 1988: bonfire night! The incident came only a few days after Frank had been too drunk to stand up on stage and having to sing propped up on a stack of beer crates in front of 500 people at Goldwyn's in Birmingham. The bus fire was the straw that broke the camel's back; he'd been fucking around for a long while and this time Dom and Jim kicked him out the band. Sideshow Fatman continued with some new guy for a few months but they couldn't really get it together again and split up a little while later. Frank remained proud of the fact that *Generation Nihilists* was now a collector's item amongst vinyl junkies. That album should have been big; it contained some of the best songs of the era. It was a pity more people didn't get to hear it. But times change, these days Frank was just a washed-up could-a-been who worked operating a slitting machine in a flexography printing factory. They mostly manufactured corrugated plastic food packaging for housing sausage rolls. He had no one else to blame for his tedious existence. Who or what could he blame, anyway? The drugs? The sleeping bag manufacturer for not making it fire-proof? The women he couldn't stay away from? The booze? The people who threw the parties? No, he didn't think so. Maybe people were right. He'd made his own choices. Maybe he really was just plain and simple Frank the wanker.

Disintegration

Jim and Dom hadn't spoken to him since setting fire to the tour bus. He'd wanted so many times to approach them about reforming. There was now even a Sideshow Fatman Myspace fanpage on the net. People still remembered them. Twenty years on, Frank fantasised about resurrecting the dream. But even though he hadn't set eyes on the guys in years he seemed to sense from afar that the wounds were still raw. And yes, he didn't mind admitting, he felt ashamed. Being in a band was the only family he'd ever known. Jim and Dom were like his brothers and he felt ashamed of the fact that they wouldn't even want to look at his beaten-up face. He'd heard on the grapevine they'd both gotten married, had children. Frank just couldn't accept conventionality. He couldn't so easily fit the template society demands of us. He lived alone in a flat above a bookie's just off the High Street in Moseley. He spent most of his time at the bar in The Fighting Cocks; though he avoided those abysmal Karaoke nights, he wasn't quite that sad. But there was no doubt about it – life was just more difficult for people like Frank.

Another Monday morning rolled around. Frank's supervisor came over sporting her usual tacky pale pink lipstick and handed him his work sheet. "Frank, we need these out by the end of today." She turned like a ballerina on her heel and walked back to her office behind the Perspex partition from where she was always stood with her arms folded, eyes scanning the factory floor throughout the day.

Disintegration

Frank tied his loose strands of hair out the way with a rubber band, put on the paper hat and sat down at his machine. Customer satisfaction was Frank's goal. Every fucking second, every fucking minute of every fucking day, 100% dedication to his duties was his singular, one life's mission, complete with a piece of shit gold fucking plated watch at the pointless, soul-sucking end of it all.

On and on. This was no life for someone who could have been someone, could have been a rock star. These are rough waters we sail, Captain Ahab, as he always told himself. He felt like ringing someone's neck. He'd stop on the way home later and get a bottle of Rum, get blasted out of his brains tonight. There was no other solution.

Already counting the hours to his cigarette break, Frank Jackson, employee number 714967 moved the scoring and slitting assembly along its guide rods into position, made a final check of the rollers and securing nuts, and engaged the clutch...

Disintegration

NEW DAWN DIES

These slow nights pass like a scalpel cutting through your flesh. There's no reprieve, not even when passing the dazzling young blonde too beautiful for mortal eyes in the murky hallway between shared bathrooms. I'd no idea what eye-candy like that was doing in a crap-hole like this. We barely ever acknowledged each other, nothing more than a polite smile and nod each time we passed. She seemed a strangely quiet girl, shy. Nothing but fleeting little nervous glances from under fluttering eyelids. I'd noticed that she was entirely flat chested but I didn't think much more about it. Some girls are. I was never a big mamma-breast kind of man anyway.

Tonight a screaming ambulance pulling up outside punctuates the monotony. The flashing blue light strobes the alley and breaches the flimsy curtains.

You can't remain transient forever. You can drink so much coffee you begin to feel like you're going to throw up. But finally, no matter what, you keep slowing down until eventually you stop. In the end your chromosomes break down and you become immobile in a world that keeps pushing on, turning unconcernedly around you. It doesn't matter, when all is said and done. You never did anything calculable.

All the time Fat Eddie is wailing in the next room. Listening through these paper-thin walls to the destruction of a man by an invisible entity is quite disturbing. It's the drugs they've pumped him full of, you see. He doesn't know where he is or what's going on. He's dying of cancer. And the delusional son of a bitch keeps wailing and shouting incoherent babble in the middle of the night as he lays sweating and rotting in his bed. His death-room stinks of decay and it seeps from under his door into the stairwell.

You've smelt death's unmistakeable aroma before. Life is senselessly cruel and from what you've seen death usually comes to us just at a time when you feel you're beginning to grow as a person. Death hangs over us all the time, waiting to teach us that it is our one and only master. All you ever want is more time.

You were just twenty-three when your brother was killed in the first Gulf War. And for what? Nobody gives a fuck. War is ultimately inconsequential. People live apathetically, in fact quite happily, under any established hierarchy. The history books are nothing but cheap words that drip from the iniquitous lips of the victorious. Terrorists and so called rogue regimes are no guiltier than our own legitimate governments.

I would never kill or be killed in the name of some scum-sucking government. Nationalism, like religion, is an illusory concept. And those who claim to be God's chosen race are fundamentally no different to those who claim to be the master race.

In the end, the only thing worth believing in is you. But these days it's as if someone else's deadened eyes peer back at you in the dirty shaving mirror propped up on the shelf amongst the few books you carry around from place to place. You're standing on the edge of the precipice, asking the question: "who the fuck am I?"

I never had any time for philosophy or its cheap-ass sidekick, religion. You get hit around the back of the swede with a house brick and it ain't never gonna feel soft like a cushion. No amount of philosophising or praying ever changed that, and nothing ever will.

There is a muffled commotion in the hall as the ambulance crew struggle with Eddie's weight but it sounds like they finally manage to stretcher the fat fucker down the stairs.

You light another cigarette, listening out for the meat wagon to take the poor bastard away for good. And then you think back thirty-six years to that summer heatwave of 1976. Flowers in the garden. A piss-yellow butterfly, fluttering in the sunshine. Childhood memories, fragmented somewhat. But everything was beautiful then. Michelle with her clear blue eyes and short skirt. That was the first time you fell in love. Everything seemed so much simpler in those days. If only you could have known it at the time. Of course, you can laugh now at how young and naive you were, Michelle and you, ensconced in your blissful childish innocence. Broke your heart when her parents decided to move away and you never saw Michelle again.

Saccharin memories dissolve, become impossible to reconstruct. We remember things as we want them to be. And you're left with only the here and now. You are alone with only a fly on the bare light bulb for company. The bastard zips around your room looking for somewhere to lay its fucking eggs. Even so, you often leave her breadcrumbs or pieces of chocolate on the old pine table near the window.

It takes courage to accept the fact you're just some insignificant little pinprick somewhere on an island in the Atlantic, on a world spinning through the vacuousness of space. None of us have all the time in the world, no matter how slowly these nights drag by. All you ask is for two years of escape. You would give your life for just two years of guaranteed beauty at the end. You just want your own lighthouse isolated from the rest of humanity, from where you can look out at a twinkling, moonlit ocean and declare aloud, "how beautiful the sea."

In one hundred years every one of us who pass wordlessly in the despairing halls of this damned flop-house will be gone and forgotten. If your sole aim in life is to leave a residue of your existence then you may as well be Jack the Ripper. It's not difficult. Life is not sacred, it's expendable. How else can you look at it? The ultimate destiny of the human race itself can only wind up one way – in destruction. Death at the hands of some genocidal force of nature. The sun going nova. The third world war. Whatever. It doesn't really matter in the final analysis. You can only hope it will be sudden and painless. In my estimation, the only escape is to drink yourself to

New Dawn Dies

oblivion. Mary Kelly, Catherine Eddowes and the rest of them would simply never have existed if it weren't for the work of old Jack. They'd have finished their lives in the complete obscurity of the cold piss-stained alleys they earned their living in. Poor, unfortunate bitches. How awful to be famous for being butchered.

The flattened cigarette stub smoulders in the ashtray. Outside you can hear them loading Fat Eddie into the ambulance and then its morbid siren fades into the distance.

New Dawn Dies

AN ISLAND SOMEWHERE

Who would give their kid a name like Seaman?

That's what his parents called him. Second name Fish. And he had a beautiful step-sister who was the complete antithesis of him called Karen Kemp. That's how I came to know Seaman.

Strabismus, I think they call it, when your eyes are on the piss, when one of them is permanently shooting off at the wrong angle.

Seaman Fish had no time for education or work, or love, or art, or music, or literature. He didn't even have any time for cinema or any television shows, or anything at all. But he had time to drink. And to gamble. He often just wandered around the streets, eye earnestly scanning the floor, especially on market day, hoping to find money so that he could get shitfaced. If anyone laid a wallet down for even a second it would be gone in an instant if Seaman Fish was about. He said he was fucked if he was gonna go out and get a job. For as long as I or anyone else could remember he wilfully lived on benefits and whatever he could sell, find, beg or steal. He even considered himself of a slightly religious bent – after finding or filching something he would proclaim that God had given it to him.

At school Seaman was the runny-nosed kid who sat at the back of the class in his big, thick glasses, one lens blanked out. They blank out one lens so the cock-eye doesn't interfere with your one good eye. Fuckeye, all the other kids nicknamed him. It kind of just washed over him, he never once reacted. The name stuck though, and he's been Fuckeye ever since. But he wasn't as stupid as most people thought, including the teachers. He had them all fooled. Playing the imbecile was his ticket to easiness. And something else about him too: he is always buoyant; nothing ever dissuades him, perturbs him or brings him down in any way. Nothing and no one could knock Fuckeye out of his wanker stride. Riches were always just around the corner in his soft-cushioned optimistic world of entitlement.

When it came to women, I'd never seen Fuckeye with one. He claimed he only liked Japanese women. He seemed to have an unhealthy obsession with them. Japanese girls are pretty as hell, he said. But even then, from what I could decipher, he only liked them with pixelated genitals.

"I never had any ambitions," Fuckeye told me. "And if I did it would be to just go away somewhere and become a fucking drug addict." He laughed. "Oh yeah, I'm the quintessential loser, totally dependent on the state. I'm a socialist's wet dream. Do you know right now I am registered as alcohol dependent?"

He smiled, but it was more like a sneer. "Oh ya, this is the land of milk and honey for us free-loaders. The stupid cunts give me an extra little bidda dosh every week for my booze. Sometimes I drink it but quite often I go down The Dogs with it though. You know... *Perry Barr.*"

Yeah, I knew Perry Barr Greyhound Track. That's where I first met Karen Kemp. She worked as a cashier there. I was once one of the sad loser bastards who didn't know much about the game. I was down there for lack of anything else to do. Karen used to make fun of how I never won anything. But she was lovely and I didn't mind because losing all the time made the attention from her worth it.

I saw her in the street today for the first time in quite a while. Karen is so beautiful, with warm, brown eyes that completely melt me when I look into them.

"Come on, give me a cuddle," she smiled, throwing her arms tightly around me.

Her body is slender but was soft, tender and feminine against mine. We talked for a few minutes and I played with her long, auburn hair as she spoke, unable to really concentrate on what she was saying.

It didn't matter; her animated presence was always pleasure enough for me. Her glittering eyes. She was chatting fervently about something or other. As she talks she always holds my forearm with such affection and leans her head close to mine, conspiratorially. Her hair smells of fresh apples and honey. I didn't hear what she was saying. I just cupped her soft, pale face in my hand and replied, "You look beautiful, Karen."

She laughed and kissed me so fondly on the cheek. Poking me in the stomach, she said, "You should ring me! What happened to the night we promised ourselves?" and she looked away shyly for a moment.

We spoke for no more than five minutes and when we parted I watched her walk away. She disappeared around the corner at the end of the road near the roadworks, probably having no idea how those five minutes had brightened my day. The men digging the road all stopped what they were doing and stared at her as she glided past like she floated on air.

There is no one else who ever seems so pleased to see me. I felt like I was in love with her just for the ray of light seeing her brings to my life. Without knowing it at the time of her embrace I later realised the light she brought to me was hope.

My life has become so isolated and dulled that I have wanted to stay silently shut in this room in a state of catatonia, forever staring at the light-bulb. Outside stars gather above like lost orphans, travelling forever alone in their telemetries, millions upon millions of miles apart until they eventually die alone in the cold black emptiness of space. You can be lost at sea, directionless, stars meaningless. But there is always an island to stumble upon somewhere.

Until this morning I'd felt like my heart was giving in. At first I meant that figuratively – referring to the heart we all have inside our heads. But then it was my real heart. I felt like I had nothing left to give and the blood could not possibly pump through my veins much longer. There was no point to my existence. I looked at my clothes hanging in the closet and knew that if I didn't do something about the state I am in they are the empty clothes of a dead man.

I have Karen's number in my phone. I want her here with me. Tomorrow I will call her and invite her over for a night of drinking wine and watching an old classic French film. Something from the nineteen-fifties. A beautiful, stark black and white one.

An Island Somewhere

Never Promise Anyone Forever

His craggy face in the bathroom mirror. It's a difficult thing to confront as you get older, he thought. To face one's self in the mirror is to confront time itself, the mortal reality of our existence. The lines engraved into Blanco's sagging flesh were becoming steadily more pronounced. Today he'd visited his father at the home – and that was never a pleasant experience. Blanco squeezed out a sliver of toothpaste onto his brush.

She was a lovely little thing with long blonde hair, big, firm breasts and shapely legs, on the cusp of womanhood; flaunting it in her short skirt. Being noticed sexually had started to empower her; you could make out her nipples through her white school shirt. Beauty instils in the female a kind of impenetrable arrogance. It's not rocket science; they know you want nothing more than to possess them and their power lies in their ability to deny you these desires. Power, of course, can have other sources. But for the female, beauty is by far the quickest and easiest to employ should they be lucky enough to be blessed with such an attribute.

This girl was going to break hearts. Knowing she and he were of different eras and he would never take her had already broken Blanco's heart. But what really broke his spirit was the knowledge that in only another one or two more years some little, undeserving teenage scrote was going to cop the lot... all her taut, youthful glory and not even be fully aware of the sheer splendour at his fingertips. Time is surely our cruellest enemy.

Christ her tits were firm and fabulous, he couldn't get it out of his mind, they led the hand down the curve of her body to that slim waist and then down between her supple thighs. He couldn't take his eyes off her and she even smiled at him as they passed each other. It was a young innocent smile and did nothing but make him feel like some lecherous ape. And then she said, "Hello, Sir."

"Oh... Susan... yes, hello." He hadn't recognised her. He was tongue-tied for a moment, feeling caught in the act.

"When you coming back, sir?" She cocked her head to the side coyly and put a finger to her lip.

"Few days that's all," Blanco shifted balance awkwardly as he rushed past her. "Just a bit of flu."

"I finished that project," Susan shouted after him.

"Yes... good... I'll, er... look at it soon as I return. Remind me!" Blanco waggled a finger at her and smiled as amiably as he could muster.

Still, even as beautiful as Susan was, her loveliness would sadly crumble away in the end, just like everything else. She could never promise anyone forever.

Who was he kidding? Things don't just end. We allow them to end. In Blanco's case nothing had ever started. He'd pissed his life away and all his relationships with women had been fleeting affairs. They hadn't stuck around. Abandoned by his own mother he was destined to seek out women who would abandon him, to behave, even, in a manner that caused them to leave him. He'd only realised it of late but this malady had been set in stone right from the day he was born.

He picked up a tin of hair wax and flung it with all his might at the wall mirror sending splinters of glass tinkling to the floor. Blanco was at the mercy of this thing coiled within him like a cancer. This knowledge of his own impending death. The sheer, unchangeable finality of it all.

There was nothing left to say, except that for the first time in his life he could appreciate the primitive beauty of the sunset and the budding stars glittering on the sea. Even the multi-coloured city lights outside his window, erupting like some sort of rare night flowers. And he was damned by the realisation that he'd left it all too late.

All these thoughts started germinating within him earlier that day; as a matter of fact it was before seeing the teenage schoolgirl in town. Susan had merely compounded it.

The stench of death, decaying flesh or whatever it is, hits you as soon as you walk into the old peoples' home. On the way up to his father's room Blanco walked through the communal area where they were all propped up in their armchairs. In the corner, separate from the group, was an ancient looking woman with dull white hair, streaked with filthy yellow nicotine stains. She was desperately calling into the void for her long dead mother: "MOM... MOM... MOM!" Her voice had taken on the awful, forlorn tone of a lost child. Her pitiful cries just went on and on, "MOM... MOM... MOM!"

No one answered. None of the rotten, indifferent nurses went over to her. She was all alone; unable to understand why her mother didn't come to her.

It took Blanco back. His own mother had died giving birth to him. For some reason he recalled how his distraught father, who never really got over the death, used to take him out on this lake in a rowing boat. It was a foreboding, dark lake, the waters black as tar. It was said to be bottomless in the sense that no one knew exactly how deep it was due to it being a submerged coal mine. Blanco remembered looking over the side of the boat at his rippling reflection in the swirling evil of the water. No swimming was allowed in the lake as there were dangerous undercurrents rushing through submerged caverns that dragged you down into their depths. Drownings were quite common there and it was in the newspapers once how someone had slipped beneath the surface and disappeared for months before their fish-nibbled remains resurfaced half a mile away.

Never Promise Anyone Forever

The memory of that lake still filled Blanco with dread. He imagined what it would be like to be sucked down and remain lodged in those cold, watery caves forever... no mother to come and get you.

Blanco walked up the stairs to his father's room on the first floor. The old boy was getting on now, his physical body withering away, only partially recovered from a stroke four years ago. But his mind was still sharp enough for the most part.

"Hello, dad," Blanco said, dropping a bag of fruit on the bedside table. His father was lying in bed, half-watching mid-afternoon TV.

"I swear to Christ, Greg," his father said despondently, waving a bony hand dismissively towards the screen. "Kids' television these days, mindless drivel. No wonder they're all such brainless twat-rags!"

Blanco put the tube of toothpaste and his brush away in the cabinet and turned off the light. As he walked out of the bathroom a shard of broken mirror pierced the ball of his foot, making him yell out and swear.

It was a woman's greatest fear, he imagined, that men will fall out of love with them once their beauty diminishes with age. In essence, maybe they instinctively know it is a fact. Oh, Gregory Blanco you fucking paedophile moron, he admonished himself – that was just him. It was him and his inability to form deeper

- 129 -

relationships. That's why that old bird in the home had struck such a painful chord in him; he was endlessly searching for the young mother he never had.

It is true that youth will always be seductive, regardless of how much they try to suppress it and tell us it's wrong. His mother was only seventeen when his then thirty year old father got her up the stick, for christ's sake. Nobody batted an eyelid in those days. If their feet touched the floor when they were sitting on the toilet – they were old enough. One day maybe current mores will shift opinion again. But for now, in his compulsive craving for youth, Greg knew he would never experience the depth of growing old with another human being.

He rolled into bed and lay there thinking about Susan, his little teenage bombshell. He reached into the bedside table for the tub of Vaseline, squelched out a glob into his palm and rubbed it vigorously between his hands. It warmed up nicely. He masturbated as he focused intensely on Susan's perfect body, shining blonde pigtails, the dark areolas tantalisingly visible through that tight, crisp white school shirt.

Afterwards he lay there and decided; he'd give the dirty little bitch an 'A' for that paper.

METAMORPHOSIS

In the hours before Fiona Budd died she was slinging back gin & tonics as she danced in Kaleidoscope.

The packed dance floor was heaving like a knot of worms. But Fiona Budd was of such beauty that even amongst that dance floor crowd she rendered all the other women invisible. She was a peroxide blonde in a red leather mini skirt and faded denim jacket. That was a firm little body. When I first saw her she was caught stark in bright strobe light; like a movie star stuttered in movement by a barrage of camera flash. She was so pretty I could have fallen down dead. Her still flowering youth emanated from her in waves of energy. The world had not yet stripped her of vitality and her burning wonder-struck eyes were still viewing life with awe and high expectations.

I was alone at the bar smoking a cigarette when Fiona positioned herself next to me and ditched another lipstick smeared empty glass on the bar.

Metamorphosis

"When you smoke a cigarette," she leaned into me and confided as the barman prepared her another double G&T. "Did you know you can see ghosts in the smoke?"

I am thirty-six and I have no desire for anything, no ambition left. I wonder what it's all for. It's true that I still feel a glimmer of affinity with the human race, and as long as there is a residue of humanity inside me there is hope. I used to feel the pain of things too acutely until I reached the point of having anaesthetised myself. But my feelings were still there somewhere, buried inside me. A shrink would surely have a field day unravelling the intricacies of whoever I'm supposed to be.

I can tell them. I am the bastard child of an empty whisky bottle. Abandoned from an early age, I am the kith and kin of stray dogs everywhere, howling in piss-stained back-streets in the middle of the night. But that is how I came to meet Fiona Budd. I walked out of Needless Alley, my cold blood trickling down my forearm from where, in the dark of the narrow conduit that runs between New Street and Temple Row, I'd torn the flesh trying to locate a vein. My veins were shot to pieces anyhow, so it didn't matter much to me. I wiped away the blood with my hand and rolled my shirt sleeve back down. I was seeing wavy lines like looking through rising heat as the serum seeped through my tissues. I was feeling a little light-headed, couldn't feel my own body-weight as I walked towards the entrance of Kaleidoscope.

Metamorphosis

The city was devouring me, just like it eventually devours everyone. I have no idea what made me think I'd be any different to everyone else, no idea what made me think I would be the only one to discover an escape, even though I'd witnessed so many others slide into the same rituals of self-destruction.

All these fucked-up people, man, with their mental illnesses. They surround me. They'd surrounded me for most of my life. The faces changed over the years but the fact they were all fucked-up did not.

I liked the elaborate black bracelet tattoo around Fiona's slender right ankle. The minute I saw her she mesmerised me and I wanted to know everything about the girl.

"Heh?" I uttered.

"Here, give me a cigarette, I'll show you." She playfully waggled her two fingers at me. I pulled a cigarette out and placed it between them, expecting to see her party trick.

Fiona sparked it up with a little silver lighter from the breast pocket of her tight little denim jacket and blew a cloud of blue smoke. "You see? There. You see? It's like faces appearing out of the fog." Her bright blue eyes were glistening. She was out of her face.

"I don't see anything," I confessed. "It's just smoke."

"Oh well...." She threw her perfumed hair back over her shoulder, paid the barman, and laughed as she spun around and walked away, drawing on the cigarette, dancing her way back into the hearts of the throbbing crowd and The Stooges' *I Wanna Be Your Dog*.

Sometimes it's hard to breathe. I spent twenty years in a drug and alcohol fuelled haze. It's all such a blur that I can't remember whole sections of my life. I wish I could remember more but my memory has been fused. I don't even remember the reasons for falling in love during brief moments of hope. I wish I could travel back and forth in time through my own life, to again experience those moments with greater clarity and appreciation. To experience again all the women I have loved when the physical sensations were new and exhilarating. But you just can't appreciate anything when you're in the middle of it all; it's only in retrospect that we can see.

And, in any case, you're someone else now. The person you used to be is gone. Most of the buildings are gone, demolished. The roads have been re-covered. A whole new generation inhabits the renamed and refitted bars. You are just a ghost in the time-line of it all, forgotten. Things that were once compatible with us are no longer so and we yearn to return to how things once were. Ultimately, life is a continual process of loss. We reside in worlds where only sad photographs survive to remind us of past days. Our blood and bones have changed several times over the decades and in each present moment we don't even know ourselves. We are in a constant state of metamorphosis.

Metamorphosis

It's deflating to realise that I've become so burned out and tainted that I cannot feel any kind of exhilaration anymore. There were experiences in life that were fucking beautiful. But now I view the world only through a shattered window pane. The sheer cold of these wandering, derelict nights have rendered me numb. The life I have lived was my chosen slow method of suicide, death being the only remaining sensation I have never yet felt, I was always hurtling towards it.

Later on that night, about four in the morning, in fact, I walked out of Kaleidoscope and saw Fiona's body lying in Station Street. There was a pool of clotted blood on the pavement. The ambulance crew had already given up trying to revive her. In a strange kind of solemnity they loaded her on the stretcher into the back of the ambulance. I stood and watched it pull away. Its siren made me shiver as it pierced the suddenly still, steel grey night, before slowly fading into nothing, disappearing into the remote concrete abyss.

It was a hit and run driver. A green hatchback had smashed into her and sped away. The pigs were everywhere and were questioning witnesses amongst the crowd that had gathered about.

"Did you know her?" One of the police officers asked me.

"No. I was just a passing ship," I said quietly. "I only met her very briefly tonight."

"By that you mean you were speaking to her earlier this evening?"

"Briefly, yes."

"The ambulance guy mentioned that before she died, she said..." The officer flipped through his notes. "She said... 'Sometimes it's just as simple and final and arbitrary as this.' Have you got any idea what she could have meant?"

"No... my guess would probably be worse than yours. Did anyone get the registration number?"

"Not yet," he flashed me a pissed-off look, "but we'll get it."

Just as I was about to walk away I turned and asked the police officer, "Did you find out what her name was?"

After a brief pause he answered, "It was Fiona." He gave a weak smile, "Fiona Budd."

Like a single petal, I thought, falling from a flower.

Some things just fuck your head up if you let them.

It occurred to me then, and I have thought it ever since: some people just aren't meant to last. This world is too harsh for them. Fiona's star was too bright. Life is a transient river and some people are just not strong enough; they are dragged along by the undercurrents and, caught in the flow, they're continually torn apart against the jagged rocks.

You walk from a club into blue frost and blue dawn light as chromium stars dwindle on soulless horizons. Street lights begin switching themselves off, and those little street-sweeping buggies begin doing their daily rounds with their yellow warning lights

Metamorphosis

flashing in your frail morning eyes. The day begins revealing itself again, like a carousel. And you look around the streets as normality returns to the world, the night is over, you're nearing baseline and you don't have any substances left to erase your sense of destitution. And nothing but nothing seems the same anymore, everything feels hopeless. Everything returns to being so utterly normal and dreary again. You want to blow it all away. You just want to get high again to anaesthetise yourself from the feelings.

What chance does peace have? Peace hasn't got any weapons to fight the violence. In the realm of mankind even intellect itself is pulverised in the onslaught of willful brute force. No talent for mental arithmetic will change matters when the school bully pulls you out of your chair. You learn that early on, and the same scenario plays itself out in various forms throughout our lives.

On the corner of Hurst Street, a plume of clinical white steam rises from a van selling hot dogs and dissipates in the night. This is a shit-stained city where rapes, love affairs, murders, gang warfare, de-flowerings of youth and hollow cell phone conversations bleed into the cool, early morning air and dissolve in the ether. And none of it matters at all.

Metamorphosis

SOMETHING WONDERFUL

Come Monday morning Steve Kowalski doubted he'd have a job to go back to. Before his meeting with Lola and Dom today he went down town and wandered about for a little while. He went in the coffee shop, the one near the flea market where the repulsively ugly head-barista had bug eyes and a receding chin that disappeared into his neck, devolving into rolls of fleshy, pink fat. The ugly swine was enough to put you off your coffee. Disappointingly, the pretty waitress wasn't on duty as an antidote. Kowalski found a table over in the corner and nestled himself in away from the enveloping chatter. He sat and drank a cappuccino and then walked back out onto the dismal streets again. It had started to rain. It'd been a while and he was desperate to fuck something.

His relationships with women had always been brief, intense affairs, cut short before any deeper feelings of love had taken root, when the sex was all passion and searing desire. He was getting older now though; it had been years since he had slept with anything young and perfect and it wasn't looking like he was going to do so again unless he paid for it. He liked looking at women for the beauty they possessed. But he couldn't muster the effort required to maintain a relationship, with all the intricacies involved. To Kowalski the rudiments of the female was a distant and unknowable thing, something he would never understand or be able to relate to. Young women looked at him at one time but it didn't seem to be the case anymore. His youth had faded and he lamented the fact that an element of his being had been lost forever.

The streets were tantalisingly full of those beautiful and carefree young girls from the university with their little skirts, flowing hair and blithe smiles. But there was a searching, desolate look in Kowalski's eyes that peered through the rain like a stray dog and repelled rather than attracted them. He wasn't just walking the streets; he was prowling them with that awful starved look in his eyes. Even the great swarm of scruffy looking charity collectors and bible-bashers who plagued the thoroughfares around the vicinity of the Rotunda avoided outcasts like Kowalski. So that was at least one positive aspect to come about from his demeanour. Kowalski despised any form of charity or altruism.

The problem with socialism was that it is essentially idealism that upholds a belief in the integral good of every individual. But the fact is that not all people are good and worthy. Some of the putrid scumbags do not have a bit of good in them. And he refused to accept that life itself was in any way sacred. In fact, in many cases, it was completely worthless and expendable. In the grand scheme of things, there weren't many who stood out as a man amongst the fleas. Kowalski realised he was often too harsh though. You have to remember that life for most people means days filled with empty hours, wasting away our lives in demoralising servitude. And that in itself does things to a man's mind.

He'd have to catch the number fifty-one bus. On his way to the bus stop he stopped and looked in the jeweller's window on Corporation Street. There was a pre-owned Omega watch for six-hundred quid. Oh, there was probably enough wealth in society to go around. We could all be wearing Omega and Rolex watches. But it isn't in the fundamental nature of man to spread the wealth around. Human beings are by nature greedy, selfish fuckers. Working class, most certainly, yet not a fucking hero amongst us.

Steve Kowalski was born into shit. The middle classes look to botox as a superficial gloss to conceal their expressions. The working class have ecstasy and heroin, or whatever might be our drugs of choice to anaesthetise us from the bastard of a life we are spat into. This is the expressionless botox generation, scared of feeling, scared of expressing a single emotion, for fear of not for one moment being a perfect acceptable image. It is life imitating a television screen. Yeah, this is a reality TV show called Shitville.

Speaking of Shitville, he'd left a nice little surprise for his boss - a glass of urine on her office desk over the weekend – just a little something for the bitch to find when she got in first thing at the start of her working week.

Something Wonderful

He shouldn't laugh. There was a time when he cared about some matters. But his boss really was an insufferable idiot. Kowalski had no idea how the woman had managed to attain her position. Of course, thinking about it, he did know. It was the same in any large corporation. It had little to do with ability. It was all spineless office politics, toeing the party line. It's a question of whether you're willing to sell your soul to the company, say the right things to the right people. Regardless of both common sense and personal opinion you just keep parroting the sycophantic company spiel. Eventually you absorb all their crap like a sponge, you actually start believing it, and you suck it all up and then sweat it out from every pore. Scratching backs was the route to success. Such things disgusted Kowalski; he refused to play the game.

When he was kid, Kowalski kept two pet terrapins in an aquarium. If he didn't clean them out for any length of time they'd begin to emit an indescribable stale, deathly smell. He didn't know what on earth could be causing it but his vile boss's breath was, to Kowalski at least, reminiscent of the dirty reptile tank's stagnant water odour. She was a rather cheerless, sour-faced creature with cropped brown hair. There can't be many women whose breath smells like turtle shit. Kowalski imagined part of her trouble was she hadn't been fucked in an aeon. A good punch up the knickers would probably sort her out; though he'd often wondered if she might be a lesbian, if that made any difference. Admittedly though, he had rather a chuckle imagining her on Monday morning going through the CCTV footage to see who'd left her the glass of piss.

So, at any rate, come Monday morning it was pretty certain his shit job at the bank was going to be out the window. As if he gave a flying fuck. As far as he was concerned his work at that shithole was done.

Lola and Dom
Attractive couple, mid 30's
would like to meet single male voyeur
Apply box No' 76.

The ad was in the personals section at the back of the local newspaper. Kowalski wrote to the box number and provided his telephone number. A couple of days later the telephone rang.

"You can watch us fuck," the deep voice said sternly. "And if you want, Lola will suck you off while I'm fucking her, she likes that. But you don't get to fuck her... you with me?"

"OK." Kowalski agreed, holding the phone to his ear with his shoulder as he poured a shot of chilled vodka.

"And we don't want no funny business. No weirdos, you understand? I ain't into touching other men or them touching me. Mostly, you just watch, and Lola will suck you off if you want. That's it. No weird stuff, we keep this a clean and wholesome exercise, you get me, brother?"

"Sure."

"Listen, I'm six-foot-five and if there's any funny business I'll pick you up and throw you straight out the window with no questions asked. I teach kung-fu, man, so don't try no funny shit with us. We don't like no weirdos coming around here. The main thing is that we just want someone who likes to watch. And we like being watched. What you say your name was again?"

"Kowalski. Steve Kowalski."

"You currently in employment, Kowalski?"

"Yeah," he slugged back a mouthful of vodka, "in administration. At a bank, you know?"

"Alright, Kowalski, you sound level-headed enough, just remember what I said. You come to this address..."

They arranged a time and Dom gave Kowalski an address in Great Barr before abruptly hanging up the phone.

Kowalski jumped off the fifty-one near the Scott Arms pub. He ambled past, peering through the window. Many of the same old beaten faces were sat inside drinking as they'd been doing for twenty years or more. None of them had anything else to do with their lives. The clouds parted for a moment and the pattering rain glittered in shafts of sunlight. In the doorway of the betting shop, leaning against the door frame, there was an old guy of about seventy-five dressed like Humphrey Bogart in a dark grey suit and cocked hat. He was jubilantly counting a hefty wad of notes. Such are the small-time dreams and aspirations of the disenfranchised masses. We all have them; we wear our delusions like a suit of armour in order to move through the world and hold onto our sanity. Our real identities are swallowed up in the mish-mash of media images until we don't know who we are anymore. We allow it to happen. Losing who we are protects us in a way. Our true selves protected by an outer shell of pretence.

Kowalski called in at the off-licence and bought a bottle of Pinot Grigio. He thought it might be polite to turn up with an offering of friendship.

Dom and Lola's place was a smart four-bedroom detached affair set a little way back from the busy Queslett Road with a garden lined with rose bushes. Big Dom opened the door wearing jeans and a t-shirt revealing muscular, tattooed arms. Kowalski was led into a plush living room with a glass chandelier hanging from the centre and was offered a big leather armchair to recline in. Muted light penetrated the thick, velvety drapes. Lola poured the wine for each of them, handed a glass to Kowalski and went and sat directly opposite him in a chair on the other side of the room. She sank into the leather chair, running her fingertip around the rim of her glass. She threw one leg over the armrest, offering Kowalski a teasing glimpse up her short, black skirt. She sat looking at him, sipping her drink seductively, apparently innocently opening and closing her legs, one stiletto dangling loosely off the end of her toes.

"Oh yes," Dom winked salaciously, eagerly trying to elicit some reaction from Kowalski. "Lola stirs the blood alright, doesn't she?" The man obviously got off on other men wanting his woman. It was a male one-upmanship thing, Kowalski thought.

Something Wonderful

Lola was a slim and petite, baby-faced little thing who looked much younger than mid-thirties with long blonde hair, big eyes and full lips. After a while she parted her legs completely, allowing Kowalski to see her stocking tops, the pale flesh of her thighs and white, silky knickers through which he could see a torturous hint of her dark cunt. She had him transfixed, mesmerised; it was as much as Kowalski could do to stay in his chair, he desperately wanted to leap across the room and ravish her.

"Yes..." Kowalski's heart was thumping madly in his chest, "...Yes... I have to agree she really does."

"Well, don't take any notice of her," Dom said, suddenly aggressive. He got up and strode across the room towards her. "She's a prick-teaser... nothing but a dirty little slut!" With that he raised his hand and back-handed her over the head, sending her sprawling across the Chinese rug that was spread out on the varnished wooden floor.

With his left hand he grabbed her by the hair, whilst with his right he reached up her mini skirt and yanked her knickers off. He forced her legs apart with his knees, fetched his huge swollen cock out and rammed it inside her, making her scream and arch her back. He banged away at her on the floor in front of Kowalski, before ripping open her blouse and dragging her by the hair across the floor to Kowalski. Dom forced her to kneel between Kowalski's trembling legs and ordered her to unzip Kowalski's jeans and suck him off while Dom banged her from behind.

Kowalski was initially shocked by the force Dom had hit the woman with. But in retrospect, he realised he'd found the whole thing thrilling. As Dom pounded away at Lola he knocked her soft mouth up and down the shaft of Kowalski's cock and he ran his hands through her lovely soft hair and onto her lovely firm breasts; her nipples were hard against his fingers. Kowalski came, absolutely ecstatic, in her mouth and it was all over too soon. He hadn't felt so satisfied in such a long time that he collapsed back in the chair, still excitedly mauling her hair in his hands, hardly able to draw breath from the whirling excitement of it all.

"This builds up for days," Lola told Kowalski as they all sat at the couple's long, oak dining room table finishing the wine off afterwards.

"Yeah," Dom continued, "it's something we have to do. And then we're sated again for a while."

"Will we do it again?" Kowalski enquired, hopefully.

"No. We never use the same person again," Lola shook her head. "Unfortunately it just doesn't ever have the same impact twice," Kowalski thought he detected a sympathetic air in Lola's manner. He hoped it wasn't because she felt a bit sorry for him. Married couples were a strange bunch.

As he left their home they saw him off at the door. Dom stood with his arm wrapped protectively around Lola's shoulders. "It was nice to meet you," she waved, both of them smiling great big smiles, as if they were waving off a family member after a pleasant Sunday lunch and a decorous game of Bridge.

It was early evening in the first week of January and it was just starting to get dark by the time Kowalski made his way home. The rain had stopped now and the beautiful setting sun was reflecting golden in the windows of office blocks.

And So We Turn To Dust

Doctor Berlitz looked down for a moment at his neatly arranged desk. He frowned quite intensely as if in deep contemplation. He looked up suddenly, his expression brightening, somewhat surprisingly so, Joe thought, although he realised all the same that this was an act the doctor had been through with other dead-on-their-feet patients countless times before. They develop a thick skinned indifference towards these matters.

"One positive aspect to take from this," the doctor beamed. "Is that you will now have months of being able to live a relatively normal, active life and – even towards the end – we've got a variety of medications these days that really will keep you as comfortable as possible."

Berlitz thrust his strong looking hands into the pockets of his white coat. "I would simply say go out and enjoy what time you have left." He stood up briskly, indicating it was time for Joe to leave, and patted him on the shoulder with a smile, "go out and do something you've always wanted to do... I dunno, shoot the rapids, abseil down the Grand Canyon or something like that. And spend some time with your family... Most people find that brings tremendous comfort."

There were damp patches on the walls of Joe's ground-floor flat. It wasn't a pleasant, homely place. But the rent was cheap and he'd lived there alone for the last two years. He looked at his clothes hanging in the wardrobe and he could see they were the empty, forlorn garments of a dead man. He laughed though, momentarily, at the pile of unpaid gas and electric bills stacked upon the telephone table. Right there was one victory at least. The robbing bastards could kiss all hope of getting paid goodbye now. Later that night, a few minutes after ten, Joe couldn't stand the tedium of the dank place any longer and threw on his coat and went out the door onto the street.

He didn't have any family. He thought about going to The Barrel Organ and just sitting against the bar with the express intention of drinking himself into a complete and utter fuck-this-world stupor. Except the barmaid there reminded him of Marie. Marie left him some time ago and had left him with a scar for good measure, a wound that had refused to heal. But there again, he had a scar from just about everywhere he'd been. He didn't want to be reminded of Marie's lovely golden hair and pink bubblegum lips. So he ended up trailing the streets aimlessly like a sleepwalker. Not because doctor Berlitz's revelation had left him particularly numb. Not because there is nothing behind the sound of traffic or the cry of a whale, or the bark of a dog echoing in the night. Not because there's nothing behind the warmth of the sun or the fact there are no Gods and he had no soul; not because there's nothing behind the eventual curtain of death. None of that metaphorical bullshit. It was because, quite simply, there was nothing he could think of that he'd always wanted to do. It was because when he looked at his face in the bathroom mirror he saw the skin loose, sagging, like it was melting and dripping from his skull. It was for no other reason than time itself had betrayed him.

This life was a wasteland and all things end in inconsequential dust. There is nothing. Everything and everyone is terminal, held in stasis. Even the stars above him did not move on their telemetries. It all seemed so fucking pointless.

Marie was a rare and fabulous thing. And he'd known from the outset that rare slice of good luck would be short-lived, a whirlwind romance. They'd both known it; they both knew that circumstances would prevail over them. And he knew when she had to leave nothing that beautiful would ever happen to him again. She made him so happy that just looking at her would bring tears of joy to his eyes. He couldn't believe that something so wonderful could have come to grace his life, someone he could share thoughts with, or even just sit in silence with, feeling that everything in the world is alright. From the moment she'd left, trembling and with tears flooding her brown eyes, Joe felt himself decaying by the minute.

"If it wasn't for my son," Marie had said. "I would never go back to that man."

And So We Turn To Dust

Marie and Joe were lying in bed for what turned out to be the last time. He had his hand gently resting on her beautiful pale breast, feeling her beating heart. Her gold wedding ring glinted in the morning sun streaking through the curtains.

And so it is that we turn to dust. He didn't want to think about it.

It was a cold night and he ambled along in his pea-coat and scarf. The November fog creeping around the narrow backstreets of Digbeth as he wandered about smelled of blood and death, probably carried in from the slaughterhouse on the other side of town, though he couldn't recall ever having noticed the putrid stench before tonight.

He'd felt for some time now that his heart was giving up. At first it was a figurative notion, referring to the heart inside his head. And now it was his real heart. It had been broken too many times. He had nothing left to give. There'd been no joy in Joe's life for a long time and he'd felt overawed by a sense of desolation and pointlessness. He could never let people get too close; he didn't like being touched anymore and even masturbation had come to feel like nothing more than a mechanical sequence of movements, as if he were in some way distanced from himself; a dichotomy of his body and mind.

Joe had resigned himself to loneliness, and in the end, found sanctuary in it. Indeed, death came as a kind of welcome release from the suffocation of his losses in life. He didn't feel especially bad about dying; in fact the knowledge that he only had a few months left was the first semblance of ecstasy he'd felt running through his veins in years. He certainly had nothing left to give but neither did he have anything left to lose, he had nothing to worry about anymore; he could do anything he liked and it wouldn't matter a rat's ringpiece.

It was as if for the first time in his life mercy from somewhere or other had been bestowed upon him, saving him the effort of standing on a bridge, confronting the final reality of his being. Still, he had to admit to a touch of sadness knowing that so much dies with us; our memories, our thoughts, ingrained into our every living, breathing, pulsing blood cell. But in the end it is as if our lives last only one brief second. Like a flash of light in the stagnant eye of a blind man.

Some scruffy punk kids were loitering on the corner of Oxford Street near the brothel. They were young and unaware of how perfect and beautiful their faces were. Blissfully unaware of their place in the grand scheme of things and the flowering potential life held for them. Sure enough, in their boredom, the dirty little fuckers would throw their existence away, just like almost all of us do.

As Joe passed on the other side of the road one of the boys hacked up a load of phlegm, his feet left the floor as he threw his full weight into spitting in Joe's direction. And a good shot it was too. It travelled from the youth's lips in a great swooping arc over the roofs of the parked cars – a good thirty feet or so – and only missed Joe by about six inches, a small pool of transparent liquid with a hard, green nucleus splattering at his feet on the pavement. The group all laughed as Joe turned his back in silence and continued walking down the street past the plethora of stinking kebab joints. The problem is too much dim-witted television; you only have to watch the bastard to see why all these kids are such a bunch of brainless twat-rags.

Twenty years ago Joe would have have gone over there and twisted the little cunt's head off. But not anymore. These days he'd come to accept humanity for what it is. Everything really was all inconsequential. In the end only ants will ultimately survive and become the dominant species, a black sea of them swarming across the surface of the planet. And the ants will not document the rise, fall and eventual extinction of the human race. It'll be as if none of us ever existed.

On July-the-first nineteen-eighty-seven, Joe was vaguely aware of the television blasting away in the corner of the ward. It was raining outside. The morning news broadcasted something about how police had unearthed the body of one of the missing victims of the Moors Murderers, Brady and Hindley. Joe was lying in his hospital bed, tissues all puffed up, pumped pleasantly full of painkillers. At the end of everything, all that mattered to him was

And So We Turn To Dust

that even amidst all the terror he had at least once tasted love. And Maria knew that he had loved her, too. He wondered where she was now and what she was doing. He hoped she was happy, he sent out his love to her, hoping it would be carried somehow on the winds.

At eleven o'clock Joe was pronounced dead. He opened his grey-lidded eyes for a brief second and sucked in air through gritted teeth and, for a moment, it appeared that he might be fighting for his life. But then his grimacing face relaxed as the pain dissolved and he smiled, welcoming the miracle. His eyes rolled in the direction of the patient in the neighbouring bed. "Hey Al..." Joe said in a delirious, morphine induced whisper, "Do me a favour will you? Tell 'em to bury me upside down so the world can kiss my brown-eye."

Joe and Al both laughed. And then Joe just let himself slip silently away.

Two young nurses were sent in and they methodically popped all the tubes and wires from Joe's pallid body. They chatted animatedly about the toga party Angie was supposed to be throwing at the weekend as they wheeled the corpse down to the morgue. In the corridor a cleaner was dutifully polishing the floor to a gleaming patina with one of those whirring, spinning buffer machines.

The green LCD display on the Coke machine flashed vacantly: *Insert Coins Now.*

END

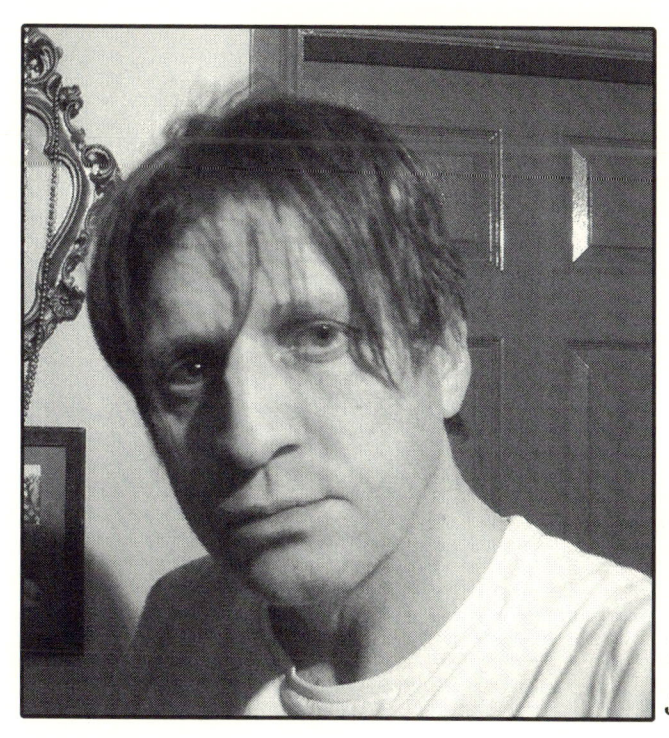

PHOTO BY u.v. ray

u.v.ray has remained on the fringes of the underground literary scene for over 20 years and his poetry, fiction and articles have appeared in numerous magazines and anthologies around the world.

His second chapbook, *Road Trip and Other Poems*, was published by Erbacce Press in 2011 and he has just completed a novella, *Spiral Out*.

THE HUNCH by Seymour Shubin

"Seymour fills his books with genuine emotion and small human touches... as well as keen psychological insights. *The Hunch* is... gripping and haunting [because] the anguish and trauma that this couple go through are genuine and heartfelt."
---Dave Zeltserman (author of *Pariah*), Introduction to *The Hunch*

"Seymour Shubin is a great crime author... [and] the novel is a delight to read."
---Rod Loft, *Bookgasm*

Trade paperback size
184 pages

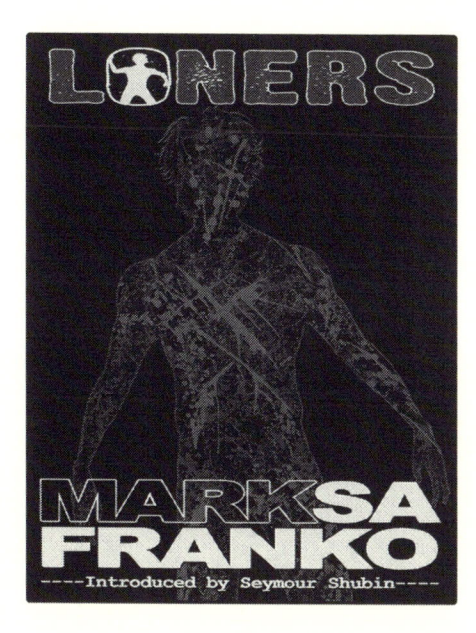

LONERS by Mark SaFranko

"Mark SaFranko dazzles with *Loners*, an addictive, wide-ranging collection of crime stories of the highest order, and some of the most compelling character-driven fiction I've read in years. Very highly recommended."
--- Jason Starr (author of *Cold Caller*)

Introduced by **Seymour Shubin** - author of *Lonely No More* and *The Hunch*
Eight pages of interior art by **Richard Watts** and **Steve Hussy**

Trade paperback size
216 pages

MURDER SLIM PRESS
www.murderslim.com

HATING OLIVIA by Mark SaFranko

"The words 'raw,' 'brutal,' 'addictive' and 'brilliant' are so overused they have almost lost their meaning, but they are fitting descriptions of a memoir from a very, very talented author."
--- James Doorne, *Bizarre Magazine*

"If you're a Miller or Bukowski fan then *Hating Olivia* is fresh meat, a gift tied together with a blood-stained bow."
--- Dan Fante (author of *Mooch*, *Chump Change*), Introduction to *Hating Olivia*

Trade paperback size
220 pages

LOUNGE LIZARD by Mark SaFranko

"With the publication of *Lounge Lizard* a ground-breaking moment has occurred... I envy the fact that you still have the jolting, pulsating, eye-opening experience of reading *Lounge Lizard* ahead of you."
--- Joseph Ridgwell, *Bookmunch*

"Here comes *Lounge Lizard*, a novel written by one hardnosed, kick-ass, American original."
--- Dan Fante (author of *Mooch*, *Chump Change*), Introduction to *Lounge Lizard*

Trade paperback size
216 pages

MURDER SLIM PRESS
www.murderslim.com

GOD BLESS AMERICA by Mark SaFranko

"*God Bless America* is strong stuff. Vomit, blood, piss. Guts. All delivered in scathing, acid prose. SaFranko does not spare the reader in this brutal powerhouse of a novel."
--- Mary Dearborn (author of *The Happiest Man Alive: A Biography of Henry Miller*), Introduction to *God Bless America*

"[It] is not only a passionate character study, it is also beautiful dirty realist fiction in the grand American tradition."
--- Matthew Firth, *Front and Centre*

Trade paperback size
278 pages

THE SAVAGE KICK #2
featuring:
Exclusive Interview with **Doug Stanhope**
Balls by Tony O'Neill
Dance of the Seven Dwarfs by Zsolt Alapi
Toothpick Whore by Peter Wollman
Exclusive Interview with **Joe R. Lansdale**
Drive-In Date by Joe R. Lansdale
and
Savage Kick's article on **Authors**

6 pages of original art by **Richard Watts**

Available in **full colour** or **black & white**
62 pages
19,500 words approx

MURDER SLIM PRESS
www.murderslim.com

THE SAVAGE KICK #3
featuring:
Exclusive Interview with **Mark SaFranko**
Haunting Refrain by **Mark SaFranko**
Wilson by **Steve Hussy**
Savage Kick's article on **Comic Book Writers**
Peepshow by **Joe Matt**
2 Days - 2 Nights by **Frank Baron**
Exclusive, 12 page Interview with **Jim Goad**
Overture: Drowning In Shit by **Jim Goad**

6 pages of original art by **Richard Watts, Mark SaFranko** and **Steve Hussy**

Available in **full colour** or **black & white**
78 pages
22,500 words approx.

THE SAVAGE KICK #4
featuring:
Exclusive Interview with **Joe Matt**
Sexaholics Anonymous by **Joe Matt**
Walk on Gilded Splinters by **Megan Hall**
Savage Kick's article on **Submissions**
Thought Crime by **Steve Ely**
3 Poems & Article on **Publishers** by **Dan Fante**
Marooned by **Tony O'Neill**
Exclusive Interview with **Tommy Trantino**
Captain Delicious... by **Tommy Trantino**
8 pages of original art by **Richard Watts, Tommy Trantino** and **Steve Hussy**

Available in **full colour** or **black & white**
82 pages / 24,000 words approx.

MURDER SLIM PRESS
www.murderslim.com

THE SAVAGE KICK #5
featuring:
Ivan Brunetti: Interview & **Cartoons** /
Another Tough Time by **Mark SaFranko** /
Deadly Spanking by **Jim Hanley** / *First*
by **Steve Hussy** / *Slut, Bitch, Whore* by
Julie Kazimer / **Seymour Shubin**:
Interview & *Lonely No More* / *Worse*
Feeling There Is by **Robert McGowan** /
Bloody Virtue by **Jeffrey Bacon** / *Carl of*
Hollyweird by **Kevin O'Kendley** /
Halloween by **J.R. Helton** / **Joe R.**
Lansdale: Interview & *One Of Them* /
SK's Picks of 2009 / Cover by **Richard**
Watts / 10 Pages of Art by **Steve Hussy**

Triple sized / 232 pages

THE SAVAGE KICK #6
featuring:
Dan Fante: Interview & **Point Doom** excerpt
Dead To Rights by **Seymour Shubin**
The First Flower by **u.v. ray**
Slug by **Steve Hussy**
Debbie Drechsler: Interview & *Daddy Knows*
Best / *The Target* by **Kevin O'Kendley**
Headache by **William Hart**
Innocent by **Aaron Garrison**
Prison Prose by **Jeffrey Frye**
Morning by **Matthew Wilding**
Things That Weren't True by **Rob McGowan**
Savage Kick's Picks of 2010 and 2011
Cover & 12 Pages of Art by **Steve Hussy**

Triple sized / 206 pages

MURDER SLIM PRESS
www.murderslim.com

NAM by **Robert McGowan**

"[*NAM* approaches its] troubling subject from all sides, chipping away at the mysterious monolith that was the American war [and] Robert McGowan displays remarkable range and depth."
---Stewart O'Nan, editor of *The Vietnam Reader*, a Vietnam War based anthology

"[A] dazzling, harsh, funny and truthful book."
---*The Veteran*

8 Pages of Interior Art by Steve Hussy
Trade paperback size
218 pages

"Reading these stories from *NAM* brings back the heart of the war for all to see and hear. That's great writing."
CAROL BRIGHTMAN

A LONG PERAMBULATION
by **Robert McGowan**

"I was deeply moved. It is a brilliant meditation on life and death. Elegantly written and utterly original, this book will surely endure."
--- Robert Olen Butler,
Pulitzer Prize-Winning Author of
A Good Scent From A Strange Mountain

"Heartfelt and utterly beautiful, yet grounded in strength, integrity, and conviction. McGowan at his very best."
--- Christine Cote, Founder, Shanti Arts.

Trade paperback size
68 pages

MURDER SLIM PRESS
www.murderslim.com

SOUTH MAIN STORIES by Robert McGowan

"It is all right to copy what you see, but it is much better to draw what you can no longer see except through your memory. This is a transformation in which imagination collaborates with memory. All you reproduce is what struck you."
--- Edgar Degas (attributed)

Seven linked stories by Robert McGowan; the late, celebrated writer and artist.

Trade paperback size
Includes Photographs by Robert McGowan
Design by Terri J. Jones
92 pages

THE ANGEL by **Tommy Trantino**

"Tommy Trantino has given us the works - from A to TZZIT. He has put it all in one book replete with maniacal illustrations as a handbook to Eternity."
--- Henry Miller

"I haven't read a book in a long time that has hit me so hard -- a book so fierce, so poetic, so wise, so heartbreaking."
--- Howard Zinn

In print for the first time in 30 years
Introduced by Tony O'Neill
Chapbook size
92 pages

MURDER SLIM PRESS
www.murderslim.com

STEPS by Steve Hussy

"*Steps* knocked me sideways the first time I read it, and further reads diminished none of its power. To read *Steps* is to see the absurdities at the heart of all relationships revealed under the spotlight's glare."
--- Tony O'Neill, Introduction to *Steps*

"Hussy treads the same broken path [as] Bukowski and Fante... Yet he has a distinct poetic voice, a voice made his own. And the music? A harrowing Waitsian blues."
--- Susan Tomaselli, *Dogmatika*

Chapbook size
62 pages

LONELY NO MORE by Seymour Shubin

"Seymour Shubin knows his way around the short story because of the deceptive ease of his prose. But as you're swept into the momentum of any given tale it's easy to overlook all of his other considerable strengths: he's incredibly perceptive, touching, funny, compassionate and versatile, among a host of other qualities."
--- Mark SaFranko, from the Introduction to *Lonely No More*

Sixteen crime and confessional stories
Cover Art by Richard Watts. Lavish interior art
Trade paperback size
128 pages

MURDER SLIM PRESS
www.murderslim.com

Printed in Great Britain
by Amazon.co.uk, Ltd.,
Marston Gate.